**THE VANNER BROTHERS,
IN THE PALE RADIANCE OF THE MOON,
CAME RIDING DOWN THE SLOPE.**

In the ghostly light they rode close together, bunched, and in the wan silveriness they seemed the great gallop of a single nocturnal beast.... Below them, partly in shadow, partly in the spectral light, a ranch house, out-buildings and corrals stood. No lights shone. Inside the house there was measured breathing and a clock ticking off the blind darkness.... In a bedroom of the house, Sam Bent sat up. He looked at the window, through which moonlight was streaming. Then he reached over and shook the bulky figure lying beside him.

"Jarle! Janie!"...

A turmoil of great, shapeless shadows surged up and across the window. Sam stared for an instant, para-lyzed, his heart clenched with terror. What the hell was coming out of the night? What?...

He could see them now. Three of them, looming about him, moonlight on their faces and gleaming on their guns.... Eyes palely glowing in the moonlight like lanterns hung far away. Yet they were not lanterns. They were devil's eyes, fiend's eyes... the glare of killers.

JAKE LOGAN
HANGING JUSTICE

PLAYBOY PRESS
PAPERBACKS

Dedicated to
RAPHAEL,
sheriff of Talpa.

HANGING JUSTICE

Cover illustration by Bart Jerner

Published simultaneously in the United States and Canada by Playboy Press, Chicago, Illinois. Printed in the United States of America. Library of Congress Catalog Card Number: 75-14618.

Books are available at quantity discounts for promotional and industrial use. For further information, write our sales promotion agency: Ventura Associates, 40 East 49th Street, New York, New York 10017.

ISBN: 0-872-16580-9

First printing September 1975.
Sixth printing January 1980.

1

From a distance the town looked sunken, half buried in a vast sagebrush plain, and it was difficult to tell what was adobe building and what was only sand.

But it was a town. And it was alive. And it had a single street which was the wagon road to Colorado.

On either side of the street adobe structures with roofs and doorways awry straggled along for nearly a quarter of a mile. Then the adobes quit and let the road struggle on.

In winter the street was a muddy mire which squished and sucked and popped in the sudden thaws. But in summer it was baked hard as bone.

Now it was summer. August. Near noon. And the sky was blue-white and blind.

Though he had ranched here for twenty years, that morning, John Dunn, the acting sheriff, had ridden into town thinking it was like riding into enemy country. He felt it in the air, smelled it in the dust that rolled toward him from the wagons that were already there. He'd heard it in the half-smothered bird cries in the piñon trees.

The air, the dust, the sounds. They seemed to drift toward him as if trouble was gathering finally, from everywhere.

And now, near noon, as he was standing under the portal of the Union Saloon, the trouble centered and faced him.

He was a big man, slow moving, with ice-blue eyes. He wore drooping killer moustaches and under the high crown of his stetson, his face looked rough as stone. In one craggy hand he held a slip of paper and he watched the small crowd before the saloon, thinking:

Sons of bitches! It's me they want. Not justice. It's me!

The crowd, a sullen, sweating group of sheepmen, horse traders, cattlemen, merchants and clerks along with their stiff, clapboard wives, stood grim and gritty with dust, uncomfortable, angry, glaring from the sheriff to the balcony above the saloon.

The whores were up there, women in colorful wrappers with wild streaming hair, a patch quilt of golds, blues, greens and straw yellows. They nudged and jostled one another, turned and twisted, swaying like chamisa in a breeze, and raucously chanting:

"Twenty-seven! Twenty-seven!

"Who the hell is twenty-seven?"

Opposite the saloon was the sheriff's office and jail, the door shut tight, the window locked.

A matchbox, John Dunn thought. Inside, an old man and a shotgun, and a bastard. All in a match-

6

box. Sourly, the sheriff smiled. And these bastards outside.

"Which son of a bitch is twenty-seven?"

The sheriff's gaze shifted. There were two other men under the shade of the portal. Damien at his right. Damien, owner and operator of the Union Saloon. Damien, dark-skinned, smooth, spotless, always dressed like it was julep time in New Orleans. A man-bitch, lounging against a portal post. Slim. Graceful. Like a new, gleaming knifeblade that had just snapped open.

Between Damien and the sheriff, hunched over a faro table, clenching papers, was the territorial judge, Henry Frye.

Dunn stared at him. The judge was shrunken, crouched inside a dusty frock coat, under a wide-brimmed hat, with square-toed boots that couldn't reach the ground! And his face. Angry. A wren's outrage always hopping across it! Damnit. That's all he was, squatting there, clutching those papers. A savage, furious, little bird. The whores jeered.

"Twenty-seven! Twenty-seven!

"Who's the hero, twenty-seven?"

The judge slammed down the papers and twisted, his body crouching even lower, tightening down like a screw.

He's near to bolting away, John Dunn thought.

"Shut your goddamn tarts!" Judge Frye cried. "You hear me? Shut them bitches up!"

Damien stepped out from under the portal and

7

looked up to the balcony. His narrow smile widened a bit and he shook his head at the women, and they quieted instantly, nudging each other, whispering, softly giggling like a low wind.

Damien stepped back under the portal and the judge yelled:

"All right! Number twenty-seven!"

The sheriff dropped his gaze. He looked at the slip of paper in his hand. The list. And all the trouble. The list. Names. People. Neighbors.

"Well?" Judge Frye screamed at Dunn. "What the hell you going to do? Read or hold up the building?"

Overhead the giggles gusted, then swiftly ebbed away.

What the hell difference did it make? Jesus or the President of the United States. He'd do just what twenty-six had already done. Leave their manure behind.

But, goddamnit, he'd started something. This was the way he'd chosen. All his doing. So he took a deep breath and in a powerful voice called out:

"Samuel Bent!"

There was a movement in the crowd as a burly man shouldered his way through. He came forward into the cleared space before the saloon, and then halted, throwing dark resentful glances at the men under the portal and at the girls on the balcony.

Sheriff Dunn watched. A dog's defiance. Like a

8

damned kicked dog! Above him the girls caught it, too.

"Show them your muscles, Sam!" they yelled with malicious glee.

"Show them your guts!"

"Then come up and show them to us!"

The judge banged the table.

"For the last time," he shouted, "you get them whores off that balcony or shut them up! I stood enough from them and from all of you! Do something, Damien, or I'll jail you, too!"

Sheriff Dunn saw the smile go out on Damien's face. Saw him start to swing on the judge. Then change his mind.

The sheriff grinned. The quick, abrupt shift. The way he shuffled cards. The way he bargained, changing directions like a whip snake.

Damien was now out from under the portal again, shooting a hard, vicious look at his girls. The shouts and giggling died. Frightened now, the girls huddled together.

"All right," the judge said when Damien stepped back. "That's better." Then he clamped his angry bird's eyes on the man before him.

"State your name and business."

"Sam Bent." Sullenly.

Judge Frye waited.

"Well?" he finally exploded. "Your business! What the hell's your business?"

"Beef." Grudging. "I run beef."

Dunn felt the voices were reaching him as echoes, ricochets.

"You any kin to the defendant, Lee Vanner?"

"Christ, no!"

"You any kin to the dead man, ex-Sheriff Buelle?"

"Not even him!" a little more confidently now, a little more defiant, remembering that friends and neighbors were behind him and they had eyes and ears and long memories.

"Well, then!"

Sheriff Dunn grinned. That bird-judge thought he was a cougar, a fox, a lion . . . crouched, ready to spring.

"You think you could render a fair judgment in this trial?" Judge Frye.

"Sure I could!"

"You could, eh?" the judge shouted. The sheriff watched him come half out of his chair, teeth bared, lips drawn back. "You figure you could?"

Curtly, Sam Bent nodded.

"Then, mister, you ready to serve on the jury?"

"Can't." Sam Bent spat out the words. "I'm busy."

Laughter burst from the balcony. The whores twisted, jostled and swayed as if a wind had caught them and their sound was shrill and mocking and raw. Sheriff Dunn heard it as if it was a faraway part of himself.

"Goddamnit," Judge Frye screamed and leaped up from the faro table. He came down off the portal in one bound, a small dark bundle. The Law beside itself with rage.

"What the hell you mean, you're busy?" He shook a fist at Sam Bent. "What the hell kind of respect for the Law is this? It is not an outhouse for you to piss in!"

That's it, Sheriff Dunn thought, and he folded his slip of paper. Finished. Over. And he felt that once again, he was beginning his own, solitary ride.

"Twenty-six men I called," the judge was screaming, gyrating about like a flail. Then he came to a stop and faced them. The town's undertaker. The sheepmen. The horse traders. The cattlemen. Shouting up at the solid, well-fed stockade of faces:

"Twenty-six substantial and respected citizens of this damn town! More'n two dozen of you bastards I called to serve on this jury! To try a man alleged to have murdered your ex-sheriff. Twenty-six! No! Twenty-seven! And what do I get? Every single stinking one is suddenly too busy to serve!"

"I got branding to do!"

Judge Frye whirled on Sam Bent. John Dunn was gazing at them as if he had already moved far away.

"Branding?" The judge stabbed a finger at the crowd. "And him? He's got inventory! And that SOB, he's got to move his horses to another pasture. And that one? He's got his old sick mother to lift and carry and feed corn mush to. You're all goddamn liars! Twenty-seven stinking liars!"

"That ain't true!"

"No? Then what is, mister? What is true?"

The sheriff tensed as if it was *his* question, as if it had been stolen, ripped out of him. Flung raw and naked and squirming on the hard mud.

"There were four men done that killing!" Sam Bent shouted, bursting with righteousness and indignation.

"Four of them! Four Vanner brothers! You only got *one* of them here in jail! The others! Still free as snakes and they all are just as poisonous and mean as the one you got jailed! We go on that jury and convict him, we execute ourselves! His brothers'll come down and massacre this town!"

"You saying you're afraid to serve on this jury?" Judge Frye demanded.

"Damnit!" Sam Bent's outrage was enormous. "They already sent word they'll murder us! Like the Assyrians on the fold they'll come down from them mountains and kill us like sheep! We got families to think about. Wives and kids!"

For a full moment the sheriff stared at Bent. Then he looked at the crowd. Once more he turned. He blinked up at the vast blue sky. He didn't feel real.

"You've got a new sheriff," Judge Frye was saying.

The sheriff looked at him. He'd caught panic in the judge's voice.

"Mr. John Dunn, standing right there. To protect you. . . ."

"Him?" Bent shrugged. "He's just one man."

"Well what the hell you want?" the judge desperately cried. "The U.S. Cavalry?"

"He's on your side of fifty. Dunn couldn't hit a horse's ass with a manure shovel!"

"Yaaaah!" It shrilled from the balcony. "How would you know? You wouldn't be nowheres near that piece of ass!"

"You'd be wetting your pants," another girl shouted, "running straight for Texas!"

The whores whooped wildly and shook with laughter.

Sheriff Dunn watched the judge carelessly. He saw his lips thin and tighten. He saw him look up at the girls, at the red lips, the bright glittering eyes, the streaming hair. And, suddenly, in the sheriff's eyes, the judge changed. A small man pinned down. Burdened by a vision of drab mud buildings, of a sullen crowd, of a baked, rutted road, all stretching aridly away. The sheriff looked to the north where the torn, jagged peaks of the Sangre de Cristos towered. He turned. To the west rose the dark, upturned bellies of dead volcanoes.

Jesus! The thought spilled silently across his mind. And we're alone. Dead alone in this damned burned-out world. Chained to and dragging this goddamn justice thing. . . .

"Never met up with anything like this," he heard the judge saying. "Never come across something like this! Nobody wanting to serve on a jury! Refusing to carry out the law!

"Damnit," the judge's voice rasped, "you know

13

what the hell you're doing? You got any idea? Do you people grasp it at all? You sons of bitches are paralyzing justice! You're laying it out, stretching it as stiff as a corpse. You're cutting the throat of the whole judicial process!"

"They'll kill us," Sam Bent protested in a thick, scurrying rage, "them Vanners you *ain't* caught, they'll come down and kill us all!"

"That!" Sheriff Dunn's lips almost blackened as he shouted out. "That might be a good thing, too!"

Judge Eve took a deep breath. Then he cried: "Get the hell out of here! This panel of jurors is dismissed! All of you bastards, get the hell away from here!"

And he stormed straight ahead, into their midst, toward the jail.

The crowd of townspeople hurried aside to let the judge pass.

And the whores on the balcony broke up into shrieking laughter, their yellow, green and straw-colored wrappers flashing in the sun, their hair wild and flying.

The sheriff looked at Sam Bent. Sam was glaring up at the girls. Finally.

"Whores! Goddamn whores!" and he spat.

2

Sheriff Dunn knew what was next. He came through the jailhouse door with Damien at his heels. The bleached adobe building was a two-room affair. In back was the jail cell. In the front half, which was Sheriff Dunn's office, Judge Frye was striding up and down.

Pop, the jail attendant, was standing in the doorway that led to the other half. He stood there, grinning out of the bony pile of seventy years, a man become beaked, wrinkled, scrawny-necked like a land turtle.

"You sure had a time out there, John," he croaked. "You got shaken like pebbles in a can."

"Uh-huh," the sheriff growled. "How's your prisoner?"

"Chortling! Chortling with pleasure!"

Furious, the sheriff marched right past Pop into the back room, knowing Judge Frye and Damien would follow.

A single cell took up the entire space and hanging on the bars was Lee Vanner. Draped like a snake, the sheriff thought. He moved toward him, feeling the hate starting up in his stomach, bringing a sour taste in his throat.

"Hear you're feeling happy," Sheriff Dunn said.

The narrow face behind the bars, with its yellow horse teeth and a crazy light in its eyes, was grinning.

"Sure am! Sure am! I heard it!" Lee Vanner shrilled. "Heard it loud and clear! No jury! Can't get no jury! Whole town's shivering and it's only past July!"

His clothes hung on him. The pants were in

15

folds, the shirt sleeves flapped when he moved. His neck and head came out of the collar like a snake straining to stay above ground.

"They're afraid of us! Yessirreee! Scared and wetting their pants. 'Cause my brothers is up there in them mountains. You fix a hanging jury and it's bang! bang! amen! goodbye! And fare-thee-well!" Vanner's voice splashed into laughter. "Bang! Bang! They'll jury you!"

"You son of a bitch!" the sheriff said savagely.

Lee Vanner squinted, the grin like a knife gash across his face.

"How's your daughter?" he said.

Sheriff Dunn grabbed the bars and his heavy face flushed red. For an instant, murderousness faced the murderer. Then he choked it down. Due process. Goddamnit! He'd get this man killed the due process way.

"You'll hang, bucko," Dunn finally said. "That's for sure. You'll hang!"

"How?" It came out of the judge like a shot.

"A rope and a tree," Damien said.

"You don't say!" The judge whirled on him. "And what about the trial? And, how in hell is there going to be a trial if you can't get a jury?"

"Listen to the judge!" Lee Vanner cried.

"Who caught this ape?" Judge Frye abruptly asked.

"I did." The sheriff shifted restlessly. "Soon after I took over. Nothing to be proud of. He was taking a bath in the Rio Grande."

16

"Caught me stark naked," Vanner giggled. "Bare-assed as the day I bounced in mama's arms. And he brung me into town with just these hands to cover my privates. All the ladies fairly died!"

Dunn could feel his restlessness climbing, rushing beyond him, beginning to pull him wildly along.

"Listen," he said through his teeth, trying to hold the restlessness down before it became sheer violence, "goddamnit, we're just wasting time."

"Wasting time?" The judge indignantly shrieked. "What the hell do you mean? It's not me who can't come up with a jury."

"You've got a circuit to ride?"

"You're damn right, I have! Got other towns waiting for me. So?"

"So when will you get back here?"

Frye stared. Then. "What the hell for?"

"For him," Dunn jerked his thumb at the prisoner. "For his trial."

"What trial? Damnit, you're not even going to have a defendant anymore!"

"Huh?" Damien.

"Don't you know what's in the Bill of Rights?"

"Never read it."

"Oh, my God!" The judge waved his hands. "And this is supposed to be a civilized community!"

He began counting on his fingers. "One, two, three, four, five, six! Article Six, Bill of Rights! United States Constitution! In all criminal prosecutions the accused shall enjoy the right to a speedy

17

and public trial by an impartial jury. You understand that?"

Warily, Damien nodded.

The sheriff stood rock-still. He was ahead of the judge now, waiting. Let him finish, he thought. Let him stretch his sight out as far as he could go.

"Well!" Frye rushed on. "If you can't get a jury, then the accused can't get a speedy trial. And, since you can't hold a man in prison for an unreasonable length of time, that means he's got to be released! You comprehend? You follow? If you can't get a jury, then this son-of-a-bitch defendant has to go free, guilty or not! So what the hell you talking about a trial for?"

"In that case," Damien snapped, "we just hang him."

"There's not going to be any lynching!" Judge Frye cried. "Not in my district. There's only going to be legal trials!"

"There'll be one. A trial, that is!" Dunn abruptly said. He turned and shouted. "Hey, Pop!"

The old man hurried in.

"Get this bastard some lunch." And Dunn strode back to his office.

"Listen," Judge Frye came hopping after him, "what in God's name you talking about? What trial?"

Damien eased into a chair. The sheriff saw his look, the narrow watchfulness. He knows I got something in mind.

And now all the restlessness was gone. He sat

18

on his desk, his body again feeling heavy and quiet.

"Fifteen times they shot the ex-sheriff," he slowly said. "Fifteen times. Him and his brothers cut the corpse into pieces with forty-fives. He'll hang, all right. He'll hang."

"But you've got to have a jury first!"

The sheriff nodded, heavily, patiently. He gestured toward the street.

"Never expected you to get a jury out there. Like Lee Vanner said, they're scared. Of the whole Vanner clan. And," he nodded toward Damien, "of him."

"Damien?"

"Tell him," Dunn tiredly said. "Tell him so he'll understand."

Damien grinned. He's eager to tell it, the sheriff thought. Pleased. Goddamn proud.

"Our ex-sheriff, Ed Buelle, he was my friend. Brought me up from New Orleans and staked me to the Union Saloon. All I got I owe to him."

Dunn could almost see it sinking down, settling into the judge.

"So that's why! That's why they wouldn't even go on a jury and declare this baboon innocent. They can't get off the hook!" the judge snapped.

"Uh-huh." Damien grinned more widely. "Then they'd have to deal with me."

For a moment more the judge stared. Then he exploded.

"Both ways! So that's it! People in this town are scared both ways!"

19

"Correct."

"Goddamnit, you'll never get a jury here!"

"Again correct," the sheriff softly said. "But, I'll get you a jury."

Abruptly he stood and walked to the window. Felt Damien watching him, following him as if he was a stranger moving steadily along some ridge.

"Not here. Can't. That's a fact." He pointed beyond the glass. "But, out there. I'll get one way out there. I'll go hunting for them. I'll go hunting for those jurors in the mountains. In the valleys. On the mesas and in the arroyos. And, by God, anyone I see riding, walking, sitting or sleeping, I'll drag 'em here. Anyone. Anything that makes a human sound. A screech, a whimper, a goddamn bellow, so long as it's got the sound of man, I'll drag 'im here!"

He turned from the window and moved on the judge, coming slowly, looming over the small figure.

"And I'll keep them, hold them here till you get back. Keep them like they were treasures! The last of the species! I'll board them, pay them a dollar a day. Even if they're just warm and just about breathing, I'll bring 'em in. Twelve men. Yessir, I'll have your jurors waiting, because one thing is for sure. That rotten bastard inside isn't going free!"

"You . . . you serious?"

"What the hell you mean 'serious'? You interested in seeing justice carried out or not?" the sheriff roared.

"Sure! Of course!" The judge suddenly felt attacked. His voice was dry, his legs trembling. "But, just go out there . . . I mean, into that country and . . . and haul anybody in?"

"That's what I said!"

Judge Frye hurriedly stepped back to where the sheriff didn't look so enormous.

"All right," he said, "all right. That's all right with me! But I can't get back here for sixty days!"

"I can bet on that?"

"You suggesting I'm a liar?"

"Haven't called you anything, yet."

"But you're damned ready to, eh? Most likely soon's my back is turned! Well, I don't give a hoot in hell, mister! You can say, shout or scream what you please! But I won't be around to hear it. For two months. Eight weeks. Sixty days! And, by God, when I get back if there ain't a jury ready and waiting, then in accordance with Article Six of the Bill of Rights of the United States Constitution, that idiot defendant inside goes free!"

And he yanked down on his hat, turned furiously on his heel and stormed out, slamming the door behind him.

When it was quiet again, Damien said:

"Well, what do you know? You been figuring privately all the time."

Dunn moved to the battered rolltop desk. "All I needed was his word he'd come back."

He sat down, huge, in the oak swivel chair. Already thinking of what he must do and how he'd

21

do it. He pulled open a side drawer. In his mind, he'd executed a wide turn and was beginning the ride up another trail. Could feel the sun on his shoulders and the rhythmic movement of the horse under him.

And he felt at peace.

Damien came up close and was smiling thinly, watching him with eyes that seemed strangely mild. Then, softly:

"You go out in the mountains. You go out in the valleys, or on the mesas, or in the arroyos. . . . Them Vanner brothers'll find you. They'll spot you. And, they'll blow your head off."

"Could go out in the night." Dunn was taking boxes of cartridges from the drawer, setting them on the desk top. "Pick up whoever I find. Then bring him back the same night or the next. Mostly use the dark. I could do that."

"You're going to a lot of trouble," Damien said.

"Maybe."

He eyed the sheriff. Dunn was bigger than Ed Buelle. But he had no style. No dash. No color. That was Dunn.

"Look," and Damien's smile gleamed wider, "give me a minute with Lee Vanner in there. Less than a minute. Half. Just ten seconds."

Dunn abruptly looked up.

"I'm a Christian man," he said. "He gets killed the legal way. Besides, he'll sweat more and I'll get more satisfaction."

22

Damien laughed. "Somebody'd think you had a grudge against Lee Vanner. A special grudge."

"Ain't we all?"

"Sure." Damien hefted a box of cartridges and tossed it in the air. "Except killing him once wouldn't be enough for me."

"Look," Damien said, "how you going to make *any* jury render an honest verdict which, in this case, is absolutely guilty?"

"I'll manage."

"With them three crazy Vanners still loose in the hills?"

Dunn reached out and caught the box of cartridges. He set it neatly upon the others and then stood up.

"Board them and keep them for sixty days. That's what we've got to do."

Standing, now he began shoving the boxes into his pockets, speaking as if he was already on his way, riding down some canyon, moving alone, yet, somehow, not solitary.

"That'll mean food. Booze. Maybe even women. All of which equipment you've got."

"And the dollar a day?"

"Out of my pocket."

"Fair enough."

"So, you see, I figure there's plenty to encourage an honest verdict."

"Plenty. But still short. There's still the Vanners scaring every Joe underground."

"Ignorance is bliss," Sheriff Dunn said. "Ignorance is real bliss."

"Huh?"

He had the boxes stashed away now, bulging in his pockets. He came away from the desk with that private journey still going on in his mind. That epic, silent ride that led toward the true meeting with Lee Vanner and toward the stinking, huddled evil of his brothers.

"I'm going to pick up that jury," and his voice lifted slightly. He was almost chanting. "In those mountains. In those valleys. On them mesas. And I'm going to let them live fat. Free whiskey. Food. Women. I'm going to keep them happy with pleasures and delights, and, nobody—you hear me?—absolutely nobody is going to tell them about those Vanners who are free. Especially your girls! They're going to keep their mouths shut. And, that'll be their bliss. Ignorance! I plan on keeping them ignorant of the fact they could get killed."

He paused, glaring at Damien, looming over him. Then he boomed:

" 'Cause if they're kept dumb and blind and uninformed, maybe then, maybe they'll be brave and render justice!"

3

Below, in the arroyo, a cook fire was still burning. To one side of it there was a hobbled burro munching grass. And on the other side was the man.

A clump of willows was bunched behind him and the fire touched willow and burro and man with a ruddy glow.

John Dunn watched. In the night it had been easy to notice the fire and he had walked his horse through the sage, halting beside the dark mass of a piñon tree. Above him was the spill of hard glittering stars. The air was cool and crickets hummed. And on the edge of it all the coyotes barked.

Prospector. That was good. They all had greed. And not just for gold. All of it. Whiskey, women, food. Driven by dreams of fabulous luck and fabulous plenty.

He would be Juror Number One.

The man wore a weapon. He could see the metallic glint of the cartridges in his belt. He might just be damn fool enough to draw and blindly fire. Best to wait.

So he waited, watching. After a while bits of thoughts and images drifted through his mind.

His wife. A dark-haired, tall woman. Dead these past ten years, now once more came out of the kitchen and walked through the ranch house parlor. He saw her coming, quietly, stately, a flow of calm silence. But he was used to that. Seeing her moving through the house. Kitchen, parlor, bedroom, into the child's room. Then into the shed, climbing down the three steps of the porch, then climbing back. Safe in her small joys, as she continued her tasks.

These were his real things, and because they were the only ones, he went on side by side with them, living with them in his mind.

The ranch. The mare turning her head toward him as he walked toward her across the field.

The dark, muscled mass of the herd galloping. The foals blindly, desperately sprinting alongside their dams. Bits and fragments. Drifted.

Then his daughter. In St. Louis now. And the child. The child! The bastard child!

Abruptly, below him, the man moved. He stood up, stretched and spat into the fire. Dunn could see the holstered weapon now. He tensed.

The man reached up, pulled down his suspenders and started to unbutton the top of his pants as he turned and headed into the willows.

The sheriff grinned. A call of nature! He dismounted, tied his horse to the piñon tree and made his way down into the arroyo.

When he reached the cook fire, he drew his gun and squatted down, waiting. The burro eyed him for a moment and then, indifferent, went back to munching. The crickets hummed. The coyotes yelped. An eon or a minute. What difference did it make in this darkness. In this night?

Time was someplace else.

The willows parted and the man came back into view. The suspenders still dangling about his knees and the holstered gun was dragging on the ground. His longjohns showed dully where his buttoned fly should have been.

The man froze and gaped, looking straight into the gun in the sheriff's hand. Under the battered brim of his hat was a grizzled, wrinkled face, gone slack and stunned.

"What's your name?" Dunn asked.

"Huh?"

"Your name, mister! Your name!"

"Goldtooth. . . . Goldtooth Charlie. . . ."

"All right, Goldtooth," the sheriff casually rose, "button up. You're wanted. You're going to serve on a jury!"

4

Rumbling, swaying like a Saturday night drunk, the Raton stage came down the narrow canyon, rushing the clatter of its iron-rimmed wheels, the creak of leather, the gunshot explosions of the driver's bullwhip down through spruce, ponderosa and aspen. Then to the lower piñon and juniper, and, finally to the cottonwood groves that ran alongside a cold clear stream in which trout darted, hid and trembled.

Buck Langley, the driver, kept whooping and firing his whip. Beside him, holding on to the seat rail with both hands, bracing his feet against the floorboard, was Tex Killey, his shotgun man.

The weapon itself, rarer and more valuable than human life, was safely jammed under the seat. If anything went flying off the stage, it would be a man, not the gun.

Usually nothing ever happened here. But boredom encouraged his malice, and Buck used this stretch to holler and blast his whip simply to spook the passengers and take his vengeance for the rattling monotony of the long ride.

They were crazily careening past the cottonwoods when suddenly, not a hundred yards away, a man appeared in the middle of the road. Buck caught the movement first, then the quick flash of a shotgun barrel, and then he heard the abrupt roar as the weapon was fired at the sky.

"Hold-up!" Buck yelled and violently hauled back on the reins. Tex pitched forward, straight at the horses' rumps. He hit the floorboards, grabbed at the seat braces and frantically clung there, the horses' behinds not three inches from his nose.

The animals were rearing and neighing in a tangle of harness and Buck was fighting them, trying to get each back on its own four legs.

Tex struggled wildly, trying to get right side up, trying to get away from the stink of those rumps. At the same time, twisting to reach the shotgun beneath the seat.

"Touch that weapon and I'll blow you in two!" The man on the road aimed his gun.

"Goddamn it!" Buck was still fighting his team. "There ain't nothing to rob! There . . ." and he stopped. There was a badge on the man's chest.

He yanked hard again on the reins, got the

horses quiet, yelled a warning to Tex and then stared down at the man below.

"Sheriff?"

"You've got eyes," John Dunn said.

Tex by now was moving back on his seat, carefully eyeing the shotgun in the man's hands. Real sheriff or not, damnit, a man with a gun was always dangerous.

"Who you carrying?"

"One passenger to Socorro," Buck gestured behind him, never taking his eyes off the armed man's face. "A religious gent, I think."

Dunn nodded. "Hand down that shotgun under the seat. Stock first."

Gingerly, Tex pulled out the weapon, and gripping the barrel, passed it down.

The sheriff took it, and now with a shotgun in each hand, he turned to the stage door. There was a man leaning out of the window watching everything with eager interest. He wore a wide-brimmed black hat, a dark coat and a spotless white shirt with a string tie.

"Morning, Sheriff. I am Samuel Ely out of Denver." And his face wrinkled in a broad, benign smile.

"Morning, Reverend." The sheriff approached the window. Samuel Ely drew back and Dunn looked into the stage.

It was true. Only one passenger. But another seat was occupied, littered with a wildly scattered deck of cards. Jack, queen, king and ace . . . deuce to ten, were flung about on the leather, scrambled as if whirled by a wind. A tornado-struck game of solitaire. Dunn stared for a moment and turned.

"That's my religion," Samuel Ely gently said.

"And you do your preaching in saloons?"

"It's where I get the best full house in town!"

Still the warm, beaming smile. Dunn grunted, pulled away and gazed up at the two on the driver's seat. He looked at their fancy boots, the shirts with the mother-of-pearl buttons, and the big stetsons.

"You Texans?"

"Sure are!" They both replied.

Dunn nodded. He didn't like Texans. Always gladhanding, but before you knew it, they grabbed something from you. Still, they were warm. Alive.

"All right, you Lone Stars," Dunn pointed at the stage, "get inside. I'll drive."

"What?"

"Climb down. Both of you. Get inside."

"But I've got to get this vehicle to Socorro! This here is my responsibility! Horses. Stage. Passengers! You can't...."

Both shotguns in the sheriff's hands jerked up.

"Get down!" Dunn coldly said. "And shut up! And get inside! All three of you are on jury duty as of right now!"

5

Somewhere in the midst of the enormous sagebrush plain, gray-blue in the morning sun, somewhere in that paradise for rattlesnakes, Meliton Atensio was digging. He was already halfway through and he stood in the roughly shaped hole shoveling and sweating and beginning to curse.

He was no longer thinking of the dead man. Cristo! Only this back-breaking labor was real. This shit of a sun. This piss of sweat streaming down his limbs.

The blanket-wrapped body was only ten feet away, comfortable under the shade of a large sagebrush. Tied and cross-tied with an old lariat so that the blanket wouldn't slip, the corpse looked bundled, packaged. Freight waiting unobtrusively on a siding.

Meliton wore a gun, an old cavalry pistol. Around his forehead, a bandana was knotted. It was sopping wet. His round, dark face, the color of earth, the earth he was digging, was grim. And his small obsidian eyes were, as usual, glaring angrily upon the gauntness of his own soul.

Caramba! The rewards of being alive! Trouble! Burdens! Misery! Shit!

The woman in Chihuahua. His sister. She'll cry and wail and beat her breast and tear her hair.

31

They'll hear her screaming all the way to Mexico City.

"Mi hombre! Mi hombre es muerto!"

Muerto. So? It's the other half of life. At least it is the side that makes dreams!

His shovel struck a thick sage root. See! Son of a bitch! Life gropes hungrily, murderously, even into here, ready and waiting to eat up everywhere.

"Cah!" he said, and as he chopped down on the root, a shadow passed across the grave.

In one motion Meliton let go of the shovel and went for his gun.

"Don't."

A tall gringo was standing alongside the grave, a gun in his hand. Shit! Life and death . . . lovers! Always together!

Meliton's eyes shifted and he saw the badge. Then he saw the moustaches and the heavy face under the wide-brimmed hat. It was strange. Cristo! As if the gun was near. Point blank. But the face was far away.

"I'm John Dunn," the gringo said, "sheriff of Blindman."

"Meliton Atensio," the gravedigger replied.

The sheriff frowned, turning his head. "I heard there were two of you."

Meliton gestured without shifting his eyes. "Under the sage señor. My brother-in-law. Muerto. Last night. Fever."

Dunn moved slowly. With one boot he pushed

the sage aside and gazed down at the blanket-wrapped corpse. He felt cheated.

He released the bush. "Where you from?"

"Mexico. Chihuahua. We were going home."

Dunn nodded, still frowning. "Too bad. I could have used you both." He squinted down at the man in the grave. Jesus, he looked like a cutthroat.

"You wanted anyplace?" he asked.

For a long moment Meliton gazed back. Son-of-a-bitch anglo! If you have a soul it makes no difference. A child of God, still, you are shit! You are suspect. A criminal of criminals!

"Why?" Meliton finally said. "Because I am Mexican?"

The gun barrel came up, a bit higher, aiming straight at his eyes now.

"For murder? Robbery or for rape?"

"Why not?" Meliton, who was really only afraid of hunger, said. "Perhaps all three, señor? I am human, too, like you."

Dunn stared. What was he, twenty-two? Thirty-two? Forty? You never could tell with them. Time and the sun did something to them. Still this was a tough one. He could feel the man's separateness, distinct and dimly impressive.

He bent down alongside the grave, keeping his gun in his hand.

"Go on," he said mildly now. "Go on, finish up. You're a pretty good gravedigger. Afterwards, I've got another job for you."

6

The land was enormous, and each day just before dawn, he rode through another part of its vastness. Wherever he was, there were always more jackrabbits, gophers and rattlers than there were men. Sometimes he came across human trails. But these were few and far between and merely hairbreadths on the land.

Still he was lucky. In the first two weeks he had already five jurors.

Each day, in the predawn dark, he came out of the ranch house, went down three street steps of the portal, crossed to the corral and saddled a horse and rode out. The darkness hid him and he moved the horse in a quick trot toward the foothills, across the sage or up the canyons, and, when the dawn broke and he thought he was clear of the Vanner brothers, he would openly begin his hunting.

But, while in the darkness, he rode with his obsessions. The memory of what had happened to his daughter and the vision of formal murder which he called *justice*. That elaborate structure through which God was to be revealed.

Hardly fourteen. Raped.

In the dark it all became vivid and intense. He could see her twisting, struggling on the river bank. He would hear the screams and the rip of clothing. He would feel the abrupt tearing pain and he sweated as he rode.

And the mutilation! The mutilation of his four-teen-year-old child. Damnit! The universe had to be appalled! Everyone had to rise up, retaliate, punish. Kill. Every single being had been the victim, had been clawed and dragged down that river bank. Everyone in the world had been abused and torn.

And, still bleeding, the human structure, society, had to strike back. Otherwise, how could one bear witness that justice was real in this world, that for justice men came together and stayed together?

That it was the existence of justice that bound them, made their communities whole.

He could go out and kill this man on his own. But what would that prove? Only that there was no justice, and only that he was bitterly, bitterly alone.

His horse stumbled. He jerked the reins and looked up. The first faint streaks of dawn were edging the sky. Beyond him, cutting across his path was a more massive blackness than the night itself. The gorge of the Rio Grande.

He dismounted and began to walk toward a gigantic jagged crack that split the world.

7

John Slocum was on the bottom of the gorge, leisurely riding along the river. He was over six feet tall, muscular and lanky, and the Indian pony he was mounted on was quick and agile. Slocum wore faded denims tucked into heavy leather boots, a red plaid wool jacket and a battered stetson.

The river, choked in by the gorge, was mud-brown with silt borne down from the southern Rockies. And, by this passage, everything was dropped, the mountains diminished, the river level itself lowered as it dug itself deeper into its bed. It was as though here everything was reaching for an ultimate bottom.

Over short, abrupt rapids, the river churned and then seemed to stop, gleaming placidly in long flat pools. On either side enormous lava walls rose in dark terraces that finally opened to a blue sky.

Slocum pulled up short and the horse stopped, scraping his shin against a jagged lava boulder.

"Son of a bitch," Slocum swore, "small horses is gonna be the death of me."

But then, he laughed. It was *her* horse. He shook his head ruefully. Small horses and small women. The things they could do to a tall man.

For a while he listened to the low roar of the rapids in the river and watched the turgid water climbing and piling up in foam. Then, all at once, he was back there in Colorado, remembering, and the roar of the river became the noise and the shouts and the banging of a piano in the Alamosa Saloon.

As if he was there right this moment, he saw that faro table and the winnings piling up in front of him.

36

He'd been on his way down from Wyoming, dreaming of the wealth and easy life waiting for him at Pinos Altos, in the New Mexican Territory. Whiskey and women and money jingling in his pocket! Hot baths! Barbers! New clothes! All the way down from Wyoming, he dreamed it, and then he was in the Alamosa Saloon, with just twelve dollars in his pocket and the faro table in front of him.

Why wait for riches still five hundred miles away? So he plumped his behind down on that chair, pulled out the paltry twelve dollars and began to play.

Two hours later he had, at the very least, seven or eight hundred, already a rich man. For once in his life he quit winners. He stood up, cashed in his chips and walked out of that saloon, feeling like a branch office of the United States Treasury. Jesus! With all that money he felt like a government, a country himself.

Slocum laughed. Small women and big winnings!

He came out of that saloon and was passing an alleyway when a gun was jammed into his back and a man was saying:

"Do something dumb, mister, and I'll blow you in two!"

There were two of them, and they shoved him into the alley and emptied his pockets. And suddenly Slocum was wild with rage and he lunged at the one nearest him. A pistol butt slammed against his head and he went down like a heavy plank of wood.

But he wasn't out. He saw the two of them race to some horses, mount, and gallop like mad out of town.

Staggering, Slocum rose, lurched back into the street, found his own horse, and not more than three or four minutes after he'd been slugged and robbed, he was on their trail.

He was so mad that he kept kicking his horse so that the poor beast ran ninety-five percent scared.

It was all open country and because he'd gotten after them so quickly, he was always near enough to pull up for a second and to hear their hooves pounding ahead of him in the dark.

Then in the first light of the dawn, he saw one of them. The man had dismounted and was frantically working the cinch on his saddle. Slocum saw him turn his head and look toward him. He dug his spurs into his horse and charged.

The man yanked the saddle clear of the horse and tried to swing up bareback. But Slocum was alongside by that time. He dived, smashed into the man and they both went wildly over the horse's back and hit the ground.

Even while they madly struggled in the sagebrush, Slocum felt something wrong. The man was too soft, too full of curves, too warm. His gasps were too high and thin.

Then Slocum was on top of him and his gun was in his hand and, astonished, he was staring at a ripped shirt and round, cuplike, naked breasts below him.

38

"Holy!" Slocum said. "Jesus Christ!"

"Let go!" The girl yelled. "Let go!"

But he didn't move. The pistol barrel pointed straight at one rosy nipple.

"You finished looking?"

"What do you know," Slocum kept muttering, still stunned, "what do you know?"

"Get off me! You're hurting me!"

"I'll be goddamned! A girl! A female crook!"

Beside the river, Slocum laughed, remembering. Those breasts, those two nipples standing up, defiant, angry, as if they were on guard. He spurred the pony and began to move on.

The girl didn't have the money on her. The way Slocum had figured it out, was that she and her partner had separated so as to throw him off their trail. He was sure they were going to meet again someplace further on.

When she'd tied up the shirt as best she could and was sitting sullenly on the ground, Slocum said:

"What's your name?"

"Go diddle yourself," she replied.

Slocum sighed.

"You been brought up real nice, haven't you?"

"Uh-huh."

His jaws clamped tight.

"Listen, I want my money!"

The girl snorted.

"Damnit," he said furiously, "tits or no tits, I'll

beat the hell out of you, you don't tell me where it is!"

"Go ahead. Beat."

Slocum's hand shot out and grapped her shoulder. "You're going to tell me, you hear that?" He was yelling now. "I never had so much money in my life and I ain't letting no pair of rats get away with it, you hear?"

But the girl only grinned.

Her face was narrow, striking, and her hair thick and dark brown. It was piled around her head. And in that narrow face, framed by the mass of hair, were two hard and fiery eyes. Just looking at her began to disturb him. Besides, he couldn't get those naked breasts out of his mind. He still saw them, soft, round, like the echo of some dim longing in himself.

He shoved her away and took a deep breath and stood up. He took firm hold of himself.

"You and your partner," Slocum said, "separated and figure on meeting later, right?"

"Wrong." And again she grinned.

It was at this point that he decided on what he had to do if he ever wanted to see the green of his money again. He hitched up his pants.

"All right," he said, "you're bait."

"What?"

"Bait. You don't show up I figure your partner might come looking for you. And, lady, when he does, I'm going to be right there!"

He tied her so that she wouldn't take off. Then

40

he caught her pony, fixed the cinch and saddled it. Afterwards, he let her mount, and in the early morning light when things looked fresh, when the whole world looked as though it was just beginning, they rode on—she, as bait should be, in front—he, bringing up the rear.

The river was widening now into broad, flat sheets of water. Overhead, turkey buzzards were soaring between the cliffs. The salt cedar along the banks were coming in thicker clumps, and sometimes, in those long flat sheets of water, there'd be a silent pop and then a widening ripple. Trout. Everything was peaceful. Slocum's pony ambled along on the bottom. Slocum still thought of the girl, his loins warming.

The way she sat in that saddle! Small, straight, tough and savage-looking. Sometimes, the thought of the money went right out of his mind as he watched the swaying of her back and shoulders. And, when he did remember the money, it was like being startled out of sleep by a gunshot.

All day they rode, slow and easy, across the rolling hills. Once when they stopped to rest, she said:

"That partner of mine. . . ."

"What about him?"

"He's going to kill you, you know."

"Or, I'm going to kill him. A dollar is a dollar and about eight hundred of them is mine."

"I do admit you've got balls."

"That plus you. Which gives me an edge."

She laughed and then stared straight at him.

"You know," she finally said, "you ain't so bad-looking, after all."

Slocum suddenly felt hot. He stood up. Who in hell was the bait for? Her partner or him?

"Mount up!" His voice was harsh. And again the girl laughed.

They rode on for another hour or two and as they came over a rise, he saw a spill of great boulders below. The moment he saw them, Slocum had the premonition that it was going to happen here. He had a prickling and tightening along his legs and a sense of alarm at being right out in the open.

He spurred his horse and came alongside the girl and the instant he did that, a rifle roared and a bullet whined past his head.

He grabbed at her, pulled, and dove for the ground. They hit the ground with the girl under him and as she struggled and rolled, she was laughing and saying, "A dollar is a dollar, and it's right down there!"

"Shut up!" Slocum yanked his belt free of his pants and began to clamp it around her wrists.

"You son of a bitch!" She started screaming as he doubled her up, strapping her legs to her arms. "That hurts!"

"I don't want you loose and in back of me."

Her shirt popped and he saw her breasts again.

"Jesus," he said, and cursed some more, and ran, skirting the edge of the hill.

42

The rifle kept bursting and bullets kept whining about him.

Slocum ran in a wide circle until he reached the farthest edge of the boulders. Then he stopped, caught his breath and with his pistol in his hand, began to creep and dart from rock to rock.

The rifle kept exploding whenever he showed himself, but then, finally, it was silent. The bushwacker had lost him for the moment, and in that silence, Slocum moved as blind and as uncertain as the rifleman himself.

Slowly, carefully, he came around a huge boulder and there, not twenty feet away with his back toward him, was a man with a gun.

"Drop it," Slocum said.

The man whirled and he glimpsed a young face, long and thin with blazing eyes. He also saw the rifle coming up. And Slocum fired.

The man pitched forward on his face.

He was astonished when he rolled him over.

"A kid," he said. "A goddamn kid!"

But a dollar was a dollar and Slocum bent, went through the boy's pockets and when he straightened up he held a wad of greenbacks in his hand. His winnings!

Now he stared at the boy for a moment. It was one thing to be a fool. But it was something else to be a young one. Goddamn idiot, Slocum thought, the world was still too big for him. He took a bite of it and choked on the mouthful. Goddamn young fool!

43

But he had his winnings and now he began whistling as he walked back toward the girl.

She was still on the ground, doubled over by the strap, like a baby waiting to get born. And when she heard him whistling and saw the money in his hands, she said:

"He's dead?"

Slocum nodded and untied the strap. She sat up, rubbing her wrists and staring at him.

"Sorry," Slocum said, "it was shoot quick or get shot first." Then he cocked his head to one side. "He was just a kid."

"So?"

"I ain't happy about shooting kids."

"Dying's certain. Now or later. So what's the difference?"

He frowned. "Didn't you love him?"

The girl shrugged.

"You can get a lover anywheres," she said.

Then she stood up, her shirt still as wide open as a barn door. The cuplike breasts with those defiant nipples were facing him. Slocum shoved the money into his pocket.

"Cover up, will you?"

Abruptly, the girl grinned and began to peel off her shirt.

"What the hell you doing?"

"I'm hot," she said. "Sweating like a pig."

She bent, yanked off her boots, rose, and then stripped off her pants.

"Listen," Slocum said, beginning to feel a tightness in his belly and moisture on his brow, "there's a kid back there. Dead."

"Sure," the girl said, "and life goes on!"

She moved toward him and small as she was, neat and chiseled like a porcelain figure, her white body seemed to come at him like a vast sea.

"Oh, Christ!" He gasped, feeling sick with a sudden weakness. "Christ almighty!" And, still not admitting it, that all this time she'd been driving him crazy, that this was what he really wanted. And that even though he'd just killed a man, he grabbed her and they both fell to the ground where they rolled and murmured and whimpered until that last, final, tearing cry.

And it must have been afterwards that she hit him with the rock and he plunged into unconsciousness.

When he came out of it he was alone, stark naked, and the money gone. And nothing else in that whole damned landscape but his pile of clothes, her midget of a pony and himself, stripped and bare as a cornstalk in November, once again as poor as dirt, once again a mendicant in the world!

Small women make a man poor!

When the lava cliffs began to fall away on both sides, Slocum knew he was out of the gorge. He turned from the river, trotted his horse up a gently rising slope and reined in. Before him was the giant sagebrush plain. Through the limpid air he saw dis-

45

tant curls of smoke, and, tracing them downwards, could make out low adobe buildings. Slocum slapped the pony on the rump. The beast bolted across the plain. They reached the Colorado wagon road, and Slocum saw a wooden sign nailed to a post. It read:

BLINDMAN
3 MILES

He turned his mount south and trotted straight on into the town.

In the broad blaze of noon, the rutted streets were empty, the buildings sunk in a baking dream. Nobody. Nobody at all in front of him. A town thrown up for a theater play that never began.

Then, abruptly, he had an odd feeling. He pulled up, twisted in the saddle and looked behind him.

People. Three of them! One standing in front of the livery stable and two more under the portal of the mercantile store. All three staring at him. Had they been there all the time?

"Morning!"

But, not a word. They only silently watched as if they were standing, far away, upon another shore.

Finally, Slocum shrugged. Stones is stones, he thought, turned, and slapped his pony on. Just ahead of him was a two-story building with a rail and a long, weathered sign.

UNION SALOON

Whiskey! He headed the pony in, dismounted and tied the animal to the rail. Then he shook himself, slapping dust from his shoulders and feeling his spirits rising. He clumped up the three steps to the portal and strode through the batwing doors.

Inside, he halted instantly and blinked. It was like dropping suddenly into gray twilight. Nothing was sharp or clear, as though everything was blurred with some clay-colored dust. He rubbed his eyes and then, object by object, he made out a long bar with a short, beefy man behind it. A stairway that climbed upwards. Five men seated around a table playing poker, making slow, measured movements with their cards. And, finally, to his right, a man near the doors, his chair tipped back against the wall, his shirt front as pale as a patch of snow in the shadows.

Finally, though, Slocum coughed and got out: "Morning!"

"Morning!" the man in the white shirt replied. But no one else responded. The cardplayers watched, their hands suspended, their eyes all merged into one wide, silent gaze.

Slocum grinned and moved confidently to the bar.

"Morning!" he tried again to the cardplayers as he passed by.

And none responded. They sat silently as if it was only a shadow going by, as if they were waiting, noncommittal, until the real man appeared.

Jesus, Slocum thought, it's like I'm walking through a goddamn big graveyard.

He reached the bar.

47

The bartender moved toward him, unhurriedly.
Slocum took a deep breath.

"Whiskey!"

"Special. Today only. Double shots," the bartender said.

"Where you from, mister?" somebody asked.

Slocum turned. The tumbler was just an inch from his mouth. It was the fellow in the white shirt, who still sat with his chair tipped against the wall.

"Wyoming," Slocum said and downed his drink. Felt it uncurl inside him. He smiled. "I'm heading south."

"Anybody tell you to come this way?"

"This is the quickest way down to the Pinos Altos country, isn't it?" he asked.

White shirt smiled and slowly nodded.

Silently, all watched Slocum as he dug into his pants pockets for his money.

"Forget it," Gully, the bartender, said. "It's on the house. Second one's on the house, too."

And he refilled Slocum's glass, all the way to the top.

For an instant Slocum stared, surprised. And, abruptly something, not the whiskey, was uncurling inside of him.

"That's mighty generous of you," he cautiously said.

"And the third. And the fourth, and even the fifth."

This, from behind him. Slocum swung around.

The fellow in the white shirt was smiling, but his eyes looked hard and shiny like ice.

"It's a fact, friend," he said, "all the whiskey is on the house."

What the hell was this? Slocum shot a quick glance at the poker players. They had changed. They were grinning now, narrow, foxlike grins, thinly gleaming in the gray, dusty air. It was as if, suddenly, they had become real. Damnit, something *had* happened! Something he had missed, something had slipped by him. What? What had come in, unseen?

He shifted as if drawing all the careless, unaware ends of his lanky form more closely to himself. Something was surely cockeyed here, out of joint.

"Thanks," he said, "but I ain't thirsty no more. Fact is, I've got to be getting on."

"Sit down, friend. Have breakfast."

"And I ain't hungry neither," and Slocum started for the doors.

"Steak, potatoes, eggs, pancakes, coffee. All you have to do is ask."

"It's on the house, eh?" He was passing the poker players.

"My name's Damien," white shirt said, "and everything's free. This is Utopia, friend. Paradise. Look."

He put two fingers in his mouth and sent a shrill blast toward the gallery above them. The piercing whistle halted Slocum. He turned his head, saw a door yanked open and a girl appear on the gallery.

49

She came to the balustrade, one hand clutching a flowered wrapper shut and the other pushing back her hair. She looked dazed, startled, as if she'd just been bounced out of sleep.

"You calling, boss?"

"Robin," Damien indicated the girl. "She's on the house, too."

Slocum stared at the girl. Then he swung back on Damien.

"There's too much free around here," and he made for the doors.

He saw Damien's hands moving. They darted downwards, under the chair, and they brought up a sawed-off shotgun. Smiling, he laid it, as if it was a pet, across his lap. Slocum stopped.

"No need to act hasty," he said to him.

"Listen," Slocum exploded. "What in hell is going on here? You all crazy?"

"I own this establishment and you're being invited to stay. To join the company. You're my guest, friend."

"That's a helluva invitation! With buckshot!"

"Sit yourself down." Damien still smiled. "Get comfortable and quiet. Have another whiskey. Have a breakfast. Have a girl. You're staying. You've got a serious public service to perform."

Slocum wasn't more than three feet away from the shotgun, which, when he thought of it later, was a lucky distance to be at for a man with an uncontrollable temper, with a weakness for unpredictable indignations and righteous angers.

"Public service?"

"That's right."

"The hell with it!" he cried, "and the hell with your Utopia!"

And he kicked. Three feet was just right for a tall man. He lashed out and his boot cracked against the shotgun barrel. The weapon spun and roared, sending a rain of buckshot into the ceiling. The girl on the gallery screamed. The tilted chair twisted, upended, and Damien went crashing down on the floor. Straight for the half-doors, Slocum sprinted.

He got just outside when Damien came through and dived, hitting him behind the knees. In a wild bundle of thrashing arms and legs they both went down.

All Slocum could think of was get loose . . . get free . . . beat him off you! Kick him off you! But get free! Get free!

He came up with Damien's arms still whipping about him. Out of the corner of his eye, above the saloon's doors he could see Gully, the bartender, charging toward them, waving an ax handle.

Blindly, desperately, Slocum swung. He hit something. There was a sudden, sharp, searing pain along his knuckles and Damien was crashing back through the doors, hurtling into the bartender's arms.

With his mouth open trying to seize air, with his eyes still wild with panic, Slocum lunged for his horse. He almost had the reins loose when he heard hoofbeats coming up fast and thunderously behind him. He turned.

A big man, on a big horse, was galloping straight down on him. Slocum caught the heavy, dangerous eyes, the moustaches, and the pistol looming in his hand.

"All right," the man shouted, "hold it! Let go that horse! Hold it!"

Later, he had no memory at all of what happened except that suddenly he was running, bolting across the rutted street, his horse rearing terror-stricken, behind at the rail.

He had to escape. From what? Slocum didn't know. First, he had to be free, uncaught. Questions, answers, that was for later.

He plunged between the walls of two adobe buildings, reached their end, turned, raced along their rears, then turned again between the next two and burst back into the rutted street once more. Behind him, cursing, galloped the man with the gun.

John Slocum saw his own horse, still in front of the saloon. And that he'd never make it. Never! So he ran again, turned again between buildings and then he was lunging, tripping, tearing through open sagebrush, aimed straight at limitless space. At the mountains and the blind sky. And behind him still thundered the rider waving his gun.

He got about a hundred yards into the sage when instinct died and he stopped. He felt the surge of incredible disbelief and wonder, and immediately

52

questions rushed in. What the hell was going on? What was happening?

Now no sound. He spun around, dripping with sweat, his heart pounding, breathing in great pulling gulps.

The big man on the horse was maybe five yards away, sitting unmoving in the saddle, the gun still in his hand. For a moment they gazed at each other, as if for years each had been aware of the other in dim dreams, in nightmares. And now, for the first time, there they were, face to face.

"What's your name?" the big man finally said.

"What the hell's yours?"

The man slowly, heavily, dismounted. Slocum wiped the sweat out of his eyes.

"Dunn," the man said. "Sheriff John Dunn."

"Sheriff?" Slocum's eyes focused. He caught the shine of the badge and, abruptly, he was enraged.

"What the hell's going on here?" he screamed. "I walk into a saloon, they won't let me out. Shove a shotgun in my guts! They. . . ."

"What's your name?"

"Slocum! John Slocum!"

"Where you from?"

"Wyoming! Going south to Pinos Altos!"

"Over twenty-one?"

John stared. He could hear birds in the sage, rustlings, chatterings, sounds as if from a world they were both suddenly dead and departed from. Then, again outraged, he charged back.

"What the hell's my age got to do?"

53

"Are you or ain't you?"

" 'Course I'm over twenty-one! Goddamnit, you blind?"

"Fine," the sheriff said, but he still held out the gun. "Then, you've got a job here!"

"What?"

"A dollar a day."

"Listen, this whole town's crazy! One guy in the saloon offers me free booze. Food. Even women. Now you offer me a dollar a day!"

"It's the same job."

"What job? What the Christ hell you talking about?"

"Serving on a jury. You're going to be setting here maybe six weeks or more."

"*Six weeks?*" Unbelievingly, he watched the sheriff calmly nod. "You're crazy, you're bats!" Slocum began shouting. "Out of your mind! Six weeks! Not out of my life! I've got to be someplace."

The gun barrel jerked up, chest-high. "Move. Start walking back to the saloon."

He hit the sheriff once. The next swing the sheriff blocked. Then the sheriff came down with the gun. The barrel caught Slocum alongside his head.

The sun's glare shattered into blinding pieces. And then, everything died. Slocum sagged and dropped into the sagebrush.

Sheriff Dunn stared down at him.

"The law'll tell you when you're free, sonny," he said. "The law . . . ," and he holstered his gun.

54

8

Up a long shelf of grayish rock, three men came riding, their ponies' hooves clattering with a rush of violence upon the morning world.

In front rode Chris Vanner, then Job, and then, whooping and yipping in the rear, galloped Billy, the youngest. Each rode bareback, each bent and crouched upon their mounts as if shrilly, joyously upon the trail of murder.

Chris and Billy were naked except for breech-clouts and high Apache boots. A bandana was twisted around Billy's head, while a broad and flapping hat was pulled down over Chris's forehead. Job wore a rawhide vest over bulging chest muscles and long Navajo leggings, blue and worn. They covered his legs and left his rump bare.

The trail of rock climbed along a mesa and ended as a giant table of uplifted granite upon which enormous boulders were tumbled. The shelf was aimed at the sky like some gargantuan broken ramp.

On the table there were Indian ruins, shattered rock walls and smashed pottery shards and glinting quartz chips from spears and arrowheads.

A thousand years ago, small men with black glittering eyes had lived here. People whose ancestors had come up, murderous and fierce, out of pithouses, and who then lived their next stage, still murderous and fierce, upon this shelf of rock. Now they were gone, dust and broken bones, but the Vanner brothers galloped through as if they were remnants of that savagery, as if they were an echoing of that abrupt violence, as if here was still, the throbbing of that blood.

Which, in a very real way, was so.

In 1810, grandfather Vanner, who had been third mate on the slave ship *Camelia*, jumped the vessel in New Orleans after smashing in his captain's skull with a marlin spike and rifling the ship's strongbox. Then, because he didn't like the idea of hanging, he made his way north up the Mississippi into what was now Kansas territory.

There, the old man became a trapper. He changed his profession, but not his ways. Grandfather Vanner killed and skinned everything that bore fur. He also took to wife a Sioux squaw, from which alliance sprung father Ezekiel Vanner.

And true, the child had a biblical name, but it didn't help.

At seventeen, Zeke married an Apache woman and dwelt with her in tepees, wickiups and caves, living amidst the stink of grease, rotting guts and drying hides as he, also, continued to lower the world population of beaver, fox, bear and buffalo.

Out of this coupling came Chris, Job, Lee and Billy Vanner. Four sons who were chips off the old block and in their veins was a savage blood that pumped with a vengeance.

During the war, the two eldest, Chris and Job, had ridden with the murderous Quantrell, and both proved their ancestry at the bloody massacre in Lawrence, Kansas.

Following the war, Job and Chris drifted apart for a while, committing their depredations separately. Then later when Billy and Lee were ripe enough, they all joined together in brotherhood, and moved into the New Mexico Territory. Here, their Indian blood further flourished. Here it reached its berserk prime.

That was almost five years ago and since then the Vanners had terrorized the country around Blindman. They survived like an eternal raiding party, a roving murderous band that never rested, living off the land, burning, plundering, killing, and upon occasion, raping.

They were a breed unto themselves.

It was as if the combination, the merging and mixing of the blood of white slavers, Sioux and Apache had exploded into a wilder kind of savagery, into a new, virulent and rioting disease.

When the Vanners came, Sheriff Buelle saw his chance to get rich. When they rustled beef, he got a percentage. When they raided a freight wagon or a stagecoach, Sheriff Bill Buelle got his cut. When they killed, he looked the other way and when they raped, Sheriff Buelle grieved, shook his head and, like an avenging angel, chased some passing or invented Indians.

A fine, profitable arrangement! Buelle was on his

way to having a fat, substantial bank account down in Santa Fe, until his greed got him killed.

It happened on a pretty summer day. The Vanners had bushwacked two prospectors who'd come down from the Moreno Valley with gold dust in their saddlebags. Afterwards, as per agreement, Sheriff Buelle waited for the Vanners at the hot springs.

A summer's day, high, warm sun, the mountains sharp and clear, jays darting through the junipers. And the sheriff lolling on the ground, smoking a cigar. And in his mind, dreams of an enormous spread teeming with market beef.

When the four Vanners arrived at the hot springs, Sheriff Buelle loosened his gun and tossed away his cigar.

"Morning, Job. Chris."

He never greeted Lee or Billy. They were the juniors. He merely nodded to them.

"Morning," Job replied.

"Come for your piece, eh?" Billy grinned and stretched across his pony's back as though it was a down-filled sofa.

"Sheriff wants gold," Lee Vanner said, and giggled, "he's got a hunger for something yellow!"

"That's a fact," Buelle said, "two men dead and I'm supposed to do my duty."

"Here it is. Your duty," Chris said, and tossed a small sack to the sheriff.

Buelle caught it, hefted it, and then regretfully shook his head.

58

"Kind of small," he said. "Feels no more'n a pinch of salt in my hand."

"Meaning?"

"It ain't enough."

Billy sat up in his saddle, the grin gone.

Again, Sheriff Buelle loosened his gun.

"We got an agreement," Job said.

"We *had* an agreement," the sheriff said. "It's changed now."

"Is it?"

"Uh-huh. I want half."

"What?"

"Fifty percent!"

"You son of a bitch," Billy said.

"Half," the sheriff grimly repeated. "It ain't so easy to protect you boys anymore. But, fifty percent will do it."

"You goddamn leech!"

Job leaned forward across his pommel.

"Mister," he said, "you been living good and high off us for years. We ain't got no love for bloodsuckers. So don't push it."

"Fifty percent or I form a posse!"

"For us?"

"That's right. For you."

Billy whooped. "Jesus! Dumb? He's dumb as shit!"

"Listen," Sheriff Buelle said in a sudden burst of rage, "don't you call me no names, you goddamn little squirt!"

And Billy pulled his gun and fired.

The bullet smashed into Sheriff Buelle's shoulder and he was slammed up against a juniper. He went into it so hard that he hung there, looking shocked and white with pain. It was his gun arm, so he couldn't go for his holster.

Billy and Lee slid off their horses.

"Jesus Christ," Billy said, "I thought he was supposed to be fast!"

"You was faster," Lee complimented Billy, "but, brother, I'm faster still."

"Like hell you are!"

"Want to bet?"

"Bet!"

They both looked quickly at Job and Job nodded.

"One," Chris said, "two—*three*!"

Simultaneously Billy and Lee drew and fired. The bullets thudded into Sheriff Buelle who hung there on the juniper.

"Again," Billy said. And they both holstered their weapons, and this time, Job counted.

Six or seven times they played the game to see which one was faster, using Sheriff Buelle as the target. And all during it, the sheriff hung there on the juniper like meat in a butcher's shop, until after the seventh time. The seventh time he slid off the branches and sprawled, bloody and unrecognizable, on the ground.

"Come on now, who's faster?" Billy asked.

"Well, it ain't the sheriff!" Lee giggled and cried.

A minute later, they were all mounted and galloping away.

Buelle lay there. Huddled, smashed, all dreams, all greed ended on a warm summer day.

Then for a while, there were still four Vanners riding together. Until John Dunn took the badge.

And then there were only three.

They streaked across the great tongue of rock and reined in, kicking up stones and sparks. The ponies viciously pulled up, screamed and reared, flailing hooves in the air as if they were fighting off their own deaths.

"Hold 'em," Billy yelled, and flung his reins to Chris. He leaped off the pony, hit the rock and ran swiftly toward the tumbled boulders. Chris yanked the pony toward him and its neck arched, watching him with rolling, terrified eyes.

Past the low, broken ruins, Billy raced, his small, wiry body in the breechclout and Apache boots wiping out time.

Amongst the boulders, he disappeared.

"Goddamnit," Job said, still fighting his horse. "Some day I'm gonna split this one's brains!" He kicked at the animal's belly. "Set, you son of a bitch! Set!"

"He ain't there," Chris said.

"Huh?"

"He ain't there."

"How do you know?"

"I know. He ain't there." Like a chant, his head

bobbing with it, Chris repeated, "He ain't there."

He was a tall man with a narrow, unshaven face and far-seeing hawk's eyes. "I dreamed it. He ain't there. Dreams always tell me right and clear. Cold rocks, it said. Nothing but cold rock is there."

And then Billy burst out of the jumble of boulders.

"No sign!" he yelled. "No sign! He ain't here!"

Across the wide table of rock he ran, leaping over the broken walls. When he reached them, he grabbed at Chris's leg.

"Lee ain't here. And there ain't no other place! He'd a come here and waited!"

"He'd a come!" Job said.

"Then they still is holding him," Chris said.

"It's more'n two weeks already!"

"They still must got him in that jail."

"What for? They can't get no jury!"

The ponies, sensing the anger, like the rising of a distant wind, began to twist and rear.

"Cut it!" Job said and smashed his fist at a horse's head. "Set! Set!"

"Shoulda let him go already," Billy said.

"Shoulda."

"Something stinks, Chris!"

"A living stink! They shoulda let him go. Git!" He flung the reins back at Billy. "We're gonna find out why. Move, you bastard! Move!"

And he kicked the animal's belly. The horse bolted forward. Job clattered after him. Billy sprang upon his pony's back, and kicking its flanks as if his

62

legs were flapping wings, he plunged the horse after his brothers. They came thundering down the ramp, down the rock shelf as though that distant rising wind was here now. As if violence had arrived at sound and shape. As if it had achieved itself at last.

9

John Slocum came up as though a second rap, another blow on the head knocked him back into life.

A barge! For Chrissakes, he was on an enormous golden barge, bobbing sickeningly, dizzily, upon a white, grayish, misty sea!

He never heard himself cry out, but he grabbed hold of fistfuls of mist to steady himself and he shook his head and the mist drained away and the golden barge became a great brass bed, and where there had been no horizons, there were clapboard walls, chairs, a washstand and a tall bureau. And beside the bureau was a girl.

A ribbon held her hair and her body was sheathed in a yellow-green cloth that flashed lengths of thigh and bulge of breast when she moved.

She turned to him, and in her yellow-green wrapper, the creamy skin and burnished hair, she was all blonde as if standing in a blaze of sun.

"What'd you say, honey?"

He realized he must have cried out.

"Don't be afraid."

"Huh?"

"What'd you say?"

Hell, Slocum thought. Oh hell! Grab something. Get hold. Join the whole goddamn thing together.

She came toward him. Warmth. Brightness. An exotic yellow-green-golden jungle approaching him.

"Where the hell am I?" he heard himself say.

"Why, in my room, honey. In the Union Saloon."

And it rushed back. The bar. Free booze. The man with the shotgun. The sheriff looming and the pistol barrel cracking against his skull.

Now he panicked. Where the devil was it? He couldn't see it. There was light, though. Golden, soft, like the silent spread of oil. But where was it coming from?

"The window!" he blurted. "Where the hell's the window?"

"Oh. Boarded up. On account of jury duty, honey. It's over there."

She pointed. Slocum stared. This time he saw a lamp shining overhead and then the closely nailed boards on the wall. For a long moment he gazed at them.

"Listen, I've got to get out of here."

He swung his legs off the bed, strode over to the door, grabbed the knob and pulled.

"Locked," the girl said. "From the outside."

"Open up!" He rattled the knob. "Open up!"

"Ah, come on, honey," she gently pleaded. "Don't make no trouble and don't feel bad. Everything's free." She moved to his side softly touching his arm. "You'll have a good time. You'll see! My name's Robin. You come on and give me a kiss."

And both her hands touched him.

He turned, grabbed her shoulder and shoved. She shot across the room, slammed into the bed and landed on it so hard that she bounced. Robin stared at him, spilled as she was across the bed, thigh and breast white and gleaming. A look of astonishment spread across her face as the words of frantic apology poured out of him.

"Well, what do you know?" Her face blossomed with a pleased wonder. She got up, and crossed the room to Slocum's side.

And she took Slocum's hand and placed it upon her breast.

There were three things before which Slocum always fell. They were:

Money up ahead.

Whiskey in a glass.

And, a woman's breast.

Slocum groaned, and once again, he fell.

Later, they were lying side by side in the huge brass bed with Robin snuggling close to him as if she was in Alaska and the great freeze was on.

"You're nice, honey. You're real nice. You're even clean."

Slocum's eyes were closed. He was still drifting away on the river of pleasure.

"You know something," Robin abruptly said.

"Huh?"

65

"I don't even know your name!"

"John," he mumbled. "John Slocum."

"Pleased to meet you, John."

"Same here."

"Where you from?"

"Wyoming."

"Where you heading?"

"Pinos Altos."

Robin stirred and rolled away. "Never heard of it. And, if I ain't heard of it, it's nowheres at all."

He opened his eyes, stared at her, and then he said, "Where you from?"

"Washington County, Missouri."

"Never heard of it. It's nowheres at all."

She laughed and cuddled close.

Robin lay back. And Slocum had a feeling of contentment, of peace, that this great brass bed, foamy with its sheets and quilt, was like an island which no one else could ever reach.

And, upon it, warm flesh against warm flesh, he felt quiet and close. Slocum stretched with pleasure.

"What do you do?" Robin asked.

"Little bit of everything. Anything that'll bring an easy dollar."

"Cowboy?"

"Too much work! I gamble some. Rode shotgun on a stagecoach once. Even been a deputy in my time."

"You born in Wyoming?"

"Nope. Kentucky."

"Oh, honey, you're a long way from home!"

Tenderly, she kissed him. "Poor baby. How'd you get so far from home?"

"The war." Slocum felt his contentment tilt a bit, his island faintly disturbed.

"You fought in the war?"

"Uh-huh."

"North or South?"

"South."

"Oh. A Johnny Reb!"

Slocum frowned. Deep down inside of him he felt that old trembling, that shaking begin. He didn't like this memory but he wasn't going to let it run him down once more. That thing, he told himself, had happened to somebody else, another fellow.

He turned, grabbed Robin and kissed her hard as if, almost angrily, to drink in this present pleasure.

"That's right," he finally said, leaning back, "a Johnny Reb. You ever hear of Shiloh?"

"I ... I ... I think so."

Slocum again sat up. The quilt was around his hips now. The memory was coming back stronger and the shaking was in his legs.

"Goddamnit! Bloodiest battle of the war! 1862! I was a kid then. Nineteen years old. Fought with the Kentucky regiments."

"Where's Shiloh?"

"Tennessee. Near a place called Pittsburg Landing on the Tennessee River. Jesus! First day we beat them good. Knocked them all to hell. Then, on the second day the Yanks came like they had everybody in the world wearing blue and fighting for them. They came swarming! Cannons blasting away. Cavalry swooping out of the woods. Regiments charging!"

Smoke and flashes of fire and the harsh crashing and thundering of artillery filled Slocum's mind. And rifle fire, like hot rain, falling in buckets. And the shouts. And the screams.

His legs were shaking bad now and Robin, startled, a little frightened, grabbed him and held him close.

"I was standing in a church near a depot of powder kegs. There were dead boys and men all around me, and fellows who were just wounded, who were crying out in their pain. That Yankee artillery was thundering and bellowing like mad. When, suddenly, a shell landed in them powder kegs. It blew me out of the war for a whole year. That blast! Jesus! That blast sent me clean out of my mind. And later, I woke up in a field hospital, raving. Shock they called it. Shock? Shit! The whole goddamn world had blown up!"

And she held him very hard, pressing her warm, safe body against his, and Slocum held on to her. After a while the memory dimmed and he was wiping away her tears.

Then she smiled when he was quiet again and she rolled away upon her back and spread her arms wide and, still smiling, she welcomed him back to love once more.

10

Later, when they both heard a key turning in the lock outside, Robin rose and reached for her wrapper.

"Pull your pants on, honey," she said, "we can go downstairs now."

She was smiling, an evening smile, a sabbath smile, and she pulled the wrapper about her.

"Come on, honey."

"What?"

"Gully's unlocked the door."

"Who the hell's Gully?"

"The bartender."

Slocum sprawled, still dazed, upon the bed. Everything, somehow, seemed ahead of him, as though events were only preparing to happen. What had been in the past seemed in the future, piling up, ready to crash down. The bar. The shotgun. The sheriff galloping on top of him, the crack on the head. The girl in the passionate sheets. They'd already happened. Damnit, they had!

Or had they?

Jesus! What had she done to him? Laying with her had juggled time.

"You can't go like that, honey. It ain't decent. Put them on."

She tossed his pants on the bed. Slocum grabbed them, pulled them over his bony, gangling legs and then reached for his shirt. Robin was fixing her hair, still smiling, beginning to hum. Her pleasures were simple, domestic and always nearby.

And abruptly, he had a sinking feeling. It descended on him like a sickness. Freedom! Freedom!

He dropped back on the bed and moaned.

"I've got to get out of here! I've got to get going!"

"Oh, come on, honey!" Her voice was bell-like, a reproach from a nunnery. "Don't spoil things. Not now!"

Down at the bar, big, buxom Miss Christy, the mulatto, was pounding the piano and singing:

"Oh Nellie was a lady . . .
A long time ago! . . ."

Her hands, brown and meaty and flashing with rings, beat the instrument as if it were Mardi Gras, as if her world was unhinged and celebrating. Her voice shouted its pandemonium. Her body, breast-heavy, hip-heavy, jiggled and bounced on the piano stool, an autumn pitchwoman, sweating in soiled satin, trying to sell jubilation.

But in the great, barnlike interior of the Union Saloon, only Goldtooth Charlie and a thin girl named Lola danced.

At a large card table were Tex and Buck and Sam Ely. Buck had a girl on his lap. Tex gazed dully into a tumbler of whiskey as if expecting something to appear out of it. Sam Ely was dealing himself a hand of solitaire.

The Mexican, Meliton Atensio, was at the bar

70

hunched over a bottle as if it was the only way he could keep close to his manhood.

Nearby, Gully was wiping glasses and opposite him lounged Damien. His shotgun lay on the bar. His hand rested on the stock. He watched Goldtooth and the girl, smiling at them from out of some strange, half-lidded sleep.

Christy belted the piano and sang. Goldtooth and Lola danced. Meliton Atensio drank. Sam Ely dealt. Buck and his girl whispered and giggled. Tex waited for his gewgaw revelation. They were all like first-comers to a party, trying to get things started.

"Boss!" Gully jerked his head. Damien turned.

Slocum was coming down the stairs. Behind him bobbed a vivid, yellow-green figure. Robin.

Slocum descended wide-eyed, nervous and alert. It had about just dawned on him he was a fugitive. The feeling was brand new and he wore it gingerly, uneasily.

When he reached the bottom of the stairs, Christy smashed into the final chorus, shattering chords into splinters and ended with a shout.

Goldtooth halted, whistled, applauded and stamped his feet. Lola grinned, fanned herself violently.

"Welcome, citizen!" Christy boomed. "Welcome to jury duty as of right now!"

Damien lifted the shotgun and strolled over. "How's the lump?" he said.

The shotgun. The spotless white shirt. What the

71

hell was his name? Then the fugitive in him grabbed it and brought it up. Damien.

Slocum felt his skull. "Still there. And I'm eager to give it back."

"You going to make trouble?"

He'd get this bastard sooner or later, John thought. But to get freedom, he'd have to move in devious ways. He kept his face impassive.

"Trouble?"

"Trouble."

"Well, I'm kind of limited," Slocum shrugged. "Since you've got the gun."

Christy exploded into laughter. Damien frowned. Behind him, at the big table, there was silence and he knew they were watching.

Damien gestured with the weapon. "Drinks. Food. All you want."

"In the interest of justice, eh?"

"Uh-huh." Damien grinned. "It sure moves in mysterious ways, don't it?"

"Like rats," Slocum angrily said.

The shotgun pointed once again. "Go on. Meet your fellow jurymen."

John Slocum sighed, deliberately, with bored indifference. Then he turned and started away.

"Just a minute," Damien said.

Slocum glanced back over his shoulder holding down the grin. Bastard! He was going to say it now. He was sure of it. It was coming.

"You owe me something," Damien said.

"Do I?"

"For this afternoon."

A great sense of satisfaction settled over Slocum.

"You mean for setting you on your ass and then popping you in the mouth?" He could see Damien's jaws harden. "You want to try and collect now?" Slocum kept his eyes on the man's trigger finger.

"He sure comes up ringing bright like a silver dollar!" the big, bosomy, brown-skinned piano player crooned.

Damien glanced angrily at Christy. Then he looked back at Slocum. "I'll wait." Damien's voice was thin, like a faint scraping behind walls. "I'll wait till the trial is over."

Slocum shrugged once more and moved on, still careful to walk easily, unhurriedly, knowing it would say something more. Behind him the piano smashed into life again.

Goldtooth Charlie seized Lola and whirled her around like a rag doll. The festivities spun again, a tiny orgy in the vast barn. Someone took his arm. Robin.

"Hey, Slocum! John Slocum is what they call you!" Goldtooth had broken away from Lola and was shoving his hand toward Slocum.

Solemnly, Slocum shook it.

Goldtooth was grinning like shriveled fruit. He pumped John's hand, then let go and pulled back his upper lip to show his teeth.

"Goldtooth," he sputtered between fingers. "Goldtooth Charlie. Yours truly!" He released the flesh and excitedly indicated his jaw. "You see it? Blazing in there like a glimpse of hell! First gold nugget I ever found. Had it stuck in my mouth! Goldtooth Charlie!"

"You sure are valuable," John mildly said.

"Sure am!" and he grabbed Lola, whirled her around, singing in a hoarse, cracked voice:

"Lord's my Shepherd,
I shall not want!"

John laughed. "Hey," he said, "ain't you kind of old for all this?"

"That's a fact, sonny," Goldtooth cried, spinning Lola around, "but I ain't doing it willingly. No sir! I'm being forced!"

And he whirled across the room.

"Loco," John said, and walked on. Straight ahead to the big card table. Sam Ely was still laying down the cards. Buck's hand was wandering up and down the girl sitting on his knee. Tex lifted oxlike eyes as John approached.

When he reached the table, Buck extended his free hand, while the other kept up its erratic search.

"Welcome to the jury," Buck said. "I'm Buck Langley. Drove the stage."

"Pleased to meet you," Slocum said. Jesus! One hand on her tit, the other in my palm!

"This is Tex. My shotgun man." Tex nodded and then, as if exhausted by the effort, slid back into his dream. "And, this here is the Reverend. Sam Ely."

Sam Ely smiled beatifically.

"Howdy." It came out like a bishop's blessing.

74

Then he went back to the cards.

John stared at him, the broad, benign face and the thick, wavy hair. Then he looked at the cards. Finally, slowly, he said:

"You sure look like a Reverend. But you sure ain't acting like one."

Sam Ely looked up. He seemed surprised.

"You mean the cards?"

Slocum nodded.

A wide, patient smile spread on Sam's face.

"Don't judge me, boy," he chided gently, "all behavior's deceiving. Sure. World is full of look-alikes, therefore they're supposed to act alike. A man looks like. But doesn't act like. Well, then, he's got to be a fraud, eh?"

"What?" Slocum was bewildered.

"That's my Bible, son." Sam slapped the deck of cards. "I read from them."

Abruptly, the girl on Buck's knee got angry.

"Oh, shut up, will you? Don't start that dirty talk again!"

"Tart." Sam said. "Lousy tarts!"

"Bless 'em!" Buck giggled and pulled the girl close, both hands searching now. "Bless 'em and bless the grandest judicial system I ever did see! You know something?" He leaned eagerly forward toward Slocum. "I'm the only married galoot in this place. Got a wife down in Roswell. But, look what I got here!"

And he buried his face in the girl's bosom. When he pulled back, his eyes were shining.

"What a difference from staring at a horse's rump all day!"

The girl grinned. Behind him, Robin laughed. She linked her arm to Slocum and he felt her lips brush his ear. But he was frowning. He pointed at the cards.

"What do you mean that's your Bible? And you read from them?"

Sam leaned back. He touched a card, and, as if he'd made instant connection with the Creator, he intoned:

"I look at the ace, boy, and I think of the One, Almighty God. Lord of the Universe! Adonai! Jehovah!

"The deuce? The Bible's in two parts. Old Testament and New Testament.

"I look at the trey and I think on the Father, the Son and the Holy Ghost. . . ."

"This ain't decent!" The girl on Buck's knee prodded him.

"I look upon the four," Sam went defiantly on, "and I think on Matthew, Mark, Luke and John. I turn up the five and I recollect the five foolish Virgins. I look at the six and I think on the six days it took the Lord to create the world. The seven? I meditate how on the Seventh Day the Lord rested. . . ."

His eyes beginning to bulge, Slocum listened and watched, experiencing wonder, awe, a sense of the miraculous. . . .

"And the eight?" Slocum breathed.

Sam smiled, wreathed in confidence and certainty.

"I think of the Eight Righteous Ones the Lord saved. Noah, his wife, his three sons and their wives . . . !"

"Jesus!" John burst out. "This feller's got something! Nine?"

"Jesus saved nine out of ten from leprosy, and no one thanked him at all!"

"Ten?"

"The Commandments! All ten of them!" Sam jabbed a finger at another card. "The jack? Reminds me of the Devil!"

Then Slocum thrust a finger at another card, feeling a mounting excitement. "The queen?"

"Easy, son," Sam shrugged. "The Virgin Queen of heaven. And the king? Ah, the king? Right back to the beginning. Back to where we started out. I see the king and I think once more of the one Lord, the King of the Universe!"

Suddenly, Robin laughed. It rattled out like pebbles being flung. But the girl on Buck's knees was furious.

"He ought to be whipped," she exploded. "That's what I say. Whipped! He ain't nothing but a cardsharp. A cheap-jack crook!"

Sam banged his open palm on the table. The cards jumped. His brow was creased in anger.

"I read still more in my cards. I ain't finished, woman! Listen, open your damned cow mind and learn! Fifty-two weeks in the year! The number in the deck! Thirteen tricks, that's the weeks in each quarter! There's four suits, one for each season! There's twelve picture cards. One for each month!"

"Christ!" John was still stunned. "This is some invention!"

"He's just a tinhorn." It was Robin this time. "What's more, I'm a better invention. Come on, let's dance."

Her hands tightened on Slocum's arm and she swung him around into her own wide and ready embrace.

Furiously, Sam leaped to his feet.

"Unhand him, you goddamn tart," he shouted at Robin, caught in a gust of rage. "The one man with a spark of intelligence and you're ready to debauch him. Drag him down to the other pigs in the trough! Release him, you hear? The one single gentleman who shows any wonder and awe and interest in how I've saved and enriched my paltry life, and you're ready to teach him to laugh at me, despise me, mock me! Let him go, you damned, stinking, shameless whore!"

"Oh my God!" The girl on Buck's knees wailed. "For weeks I been listening to this. Mister, excuse me!"

She sprang off Buck's lap, hauled her arm back and swung. The blow caught Sam flush on the jaw. He crashed back against his chair, sent it skittering across the room, as he himself slammed down hard on the floor.

78

Damien, at the bar, jerked up his shotgun and waited.

"Whore!" Sam screamed. They'd begun laughing at him as he sat flat-assed on the floor. "Whore!" His knees struggled. He was trying to get up, but for a moment could not. Then, suddenly all effort stopped. He gazed up in a kind of frenzied despair.

It flashed through Slocum's mind that he was going to cry.

Sam dropped his head into his hands and sobbed.

"Bed wetter!" Buck's girl spat with contempt. Then she plumped herself down on Buck's lap and back to his eager hands.

"Now, maybe we can dance." Robin pulled on John's arm.

But Slocum didn't move. He gazed down at Sam. Heard the harsh, ugly sounds of the weeping man, the grown man sobbing.

"Come on, Slocum." Robin.

"I think I want a drink," he said. He pulled free and headed for the bar. Annoyed, Robin followed.

Meliton Atensio, a half-empty bottle at his elbow, was finishing a drink when Slocum came up. There was a mirror opposite, and in it, Meliton watched the gringo over the rim of his glass, his eyes wide, flat and fixed. He watched the figure coming at him out of the mirror as if it was death again, in another disguise.

Slocum halted beside him and reached for the bottle.

"No!"

Meliton slammed his glass down and grabbed Slocum's wrist.

"Just want a drink. That's all," Slocum said, astonished.

"Is my bottle!"

The black, glittering eyes stared at Slocum, revealing the bottom of murder. He's crazy, Slocum thought, alarmed. Immediately he let go.

"Fresh one," Gully said as he slid smoothly up to them. He planted a full, new bottle on the bar. "Help yourself." Then Gully drifted away.

Shaking a little, Slocum tilted the bottle and poured two drinks. He jerked his head toward Robin.

"What's the matter with him?"

"Sad," Robin said. "Always sad. Stuck in his misery. Well, here's to jury duty and who it brings together!"

And she drank. Slowly, Slocum raised his glass and drank.

The whiskey, warmly welcomed in his belly, stretched like a sleeping, smiling child. He leaned back against the bar, something between him and all this strangeness now.

Christy began another tune, not banging away now, but just touching the keys, feeling them as though groping for something that was still vague.

"I've gone away . . . for a thousand miles . . . But, I'm a comin' home to you. . . ."

The song, poignant, filled with longing, arched over the room, an echoing of lost and lonely things.

And Slocum thought of freedom, of wandering, moving southwards, twisting, turning, trickling down like some mountain stream in summer.

They always found their way, these streams, under deadfalls, past boulders, through slides, always they spilled on, descending the enormous land, spreading finally, somewhere in great alluvial fans.

Slocum looked toward the table. Sam Ely had risen, gathered his chair and his cards, and was sitting, staring, as if he too was far away. Tex was slouched, sunk in a heavier sullenness. Buck and the girl leaned together, cheek to cheek, listening, their faces clouded with distant questions.

"I've gone away . . . for a thousand miles.

But I'm comin' back to you. . . ."

Abruptly, Meliton hurled his glass at the mirror behind the bar. It shattered like a gunshot.

Instantly the song stopped.

"I am not dirt!" Meliton shouted, turning on the room. "I am not nothing because I am Mexican!" His hands gripped the bar behind him as though part of him was trying to hold back his rage. "I am not forgotten! Niente! A stinking turd!"

"Calm down," Gully said, moving along the bar. "Take it easy, hombre."

"Shit!" Meliton shouted it at Gully now. "Am I not on the jury? Am I not also to judge? Am I not equal then?"

"Sure. Just cool off."

"No woman! None will talk with me. Come with me. Because . . . why? I am Mexican! My blood is

81

a poison! A disease! Bitches! Whores! But they sing about love! They cut the heart with songs of love!"

And he whirled and lunged at Robin.

"You! Goddamn, I take you! You come, now!"

"Get your hands off me, greaser!" Robin yanked free.

"Bitch! Gringo bitch!" Meliton screamed.

"Now, hold on a minute, amigo," Slocum stepped in front of Robin, "a lento a bago. . . ."

"Get away, Gringo!" and he shoved Slocum aside. John staggered, tripped and sprawled. Meliton grabbed up the bottle at his elbow, smashed it against the bar, and, gripping the jagged, murderous neck, moved on Robin.

"I cut your heart out! Damn! Is no good! Dried! Is sand! Is dead! Not human! I cut the goddamn thing out!"

He lunged at her. Gully leaped over the bar. Damien, shotgun raised, moved up. But Slocum was closer. He thrust his leg out. Meliton hit it and went crashing to the floor. When he got up, the bottle still in his hand, John was facing him.

"Pigs!" Meliton screamed. "I kill you all! I clean the world. I make it all pure again!"

He charged at Slocum, the bottle raised.

John stood still. This was the one thing he knew. Was sure of. When death was actually in front of you, you stood still, you met insane, irrational, hurricane violence with a cold clear brain and a stupid fortitude.

Meliton was a foot away when Slocum knocked the glass-weaponed arm aside. Then he arced a blow from the floor. It caught Meliton flush on the chin.

The Mexican came off the ground, arms and legs spread-eagling wildly, a hawk shotgunned in mid-flight. He hit the bar and slammed down on the floor. He lay there outstretched, crucified beside a spittoon. He lay very still. Emptied of all violence.

For a moment there was silence in the room. Then, one by one, they all gathered about the unmoving Meliton.

Slocum's hand hurt. And again he had that sick feeling. It was the fallen, motionless man on the floor who had all the dignity.

"Water," Slocum said, rubbing his knuckles.

Gully brought it. John took the bucket and dumped it over the Mexican. Meliton sat up with a spasmodic jerk. He squatted down beside him.

"You all right, amigo?"

Dazed, glassy-eyed, dripping water like some thing brought up from the sea, Meliton stared at Slocum.

He's lost, John thought. He doesn't know where he is or why he's here. How he even got here.

Abruptly, Meliton seized Slocum's hand, clutching it as if his very soul had contracted in sudden dread. As though in front of him the apparition of Death had shot up, gray and mountainous.

"Padre!" he cried in terror. "Padre! Confess me! My soul is sick. I am a lost man! Confess me, padre! Confess me, I have sinned!"

And somebody said: "What the hell's going on here?"

They all turned.

Sheriff Dunn was standing in the doorway, a pistol in his hand. Beside him swayed a bear of a man, fat, huge, covered in greasy buckskins, a battered hat on his head and his face a bush of beard. Between hat and beard, though, small intelligent eyes glittered with excitement.

"Well," Dunn repeated, "what is it?"

"Nothing. It's all over."

The sheriff looked at Damien and then at the man on the floor. Abruptly, the fat man's excitement broke loose. He grabbed Dunn's arm.

"This it, Sheriff?" His voice hurried like rushing thunder. "Goddamn, is it? Is it?"

The sheriff pulled his arm free and gestured toward the bar. Instantly, the fat man surged forward. He came as though he was a storm. He came mammothlike, overwhelming, bringing with him the stink of rancid grease, of drying hides, of guts rotting in the mountain sun, of raw death still bloody from skinnings and hacked meat.

He got to the bar, grabbed up a whiskey bottle and raised it to his lips. Suddenly, though, he paused and his small ferret eyes darted about with cunning and suspicion.

84

"Monty's my name," he rumbled. "Hunting's my game!"

Then he laughed briefly, snapped it off and again warily waited. The ferret eyes probed. He grabbed Lola and pulled her up against his side. It was the last test.

"My God," she cried, "you stink!"

She struggled against him, but no one else moved.

"Damnit," Monty suddenly roared as all suspicion faded, "it's true! Holy cow! Booze and women! It's the land of the free, goddamn at last!"

And he squeezed Lola hard and thirstily drank.

Like the others, Slocum was staring at Monty. Then, suddenly, he remembered. He sprang to his feet and charged at the sheriff.

"You!" His outrage ran ahead of you. "You slugged me!"

"I apologize." The sheriff turned to go.

"Wait a minute! You ain't taking off, badge or no badge. You're going to listen to me. I don't want no part of this jury. I ain't hanging around here for no six weeks!"

"No?"

"You're goddamn right. No!"

"Well, you've got no choice. You've got a public duty to perform."

"Public duty? To get slugged? To get hauled in here like I'm a criminal? A lousy outlaw? To be held against my will?"

He was holding the sheriff's arm now.

"Get your hands off me," Dunn said.

"Damnit, man, I'm goin'."

"Let go!"

And the sheriff shoved. John went staggering back, hitting a table. He steadied himself. Then he came charging back. But Damien grabbed him from the rear, wrapping both arms about him, the shotgun barrel ending up right under Slocum's nose. Still he struggled.

"I ain't staying! I'm getting out!"

Calmly, the sheriff came up to him, raising his revolver. Still Slocum fought.

"You got no right," he yelled.

"Don't make no trouble or I'll rap you again!"

Slocum twisted violently and suddenly he was free. He swung blindly. He hit Damien and then he was crouching, fists raised, like a gangling, Ichabod rooster, ready to take on all.

"Come on, you bastards," he circled, bobbing, his long body going up and down.

Dunn raised his weapon. Then, irritated, he changed his mind.

"Get him upstairs. Lock him in. Damnit, he's crazy! Just get him out of my sight!"

A gun butt crashed behind his left ear. He was grabbed from behind again. But this time the embrace was enormous, enveloping, a hug that lifted him right off the floor. Startled, he tried to turn his head, and then he smelled it. The stink of blood and dried grease and dung, fetid and choking.

"This way!" a girl was shouting. "Follow me! This way!"

86

"You're going bye-bye," Monty's voice boomed, " 'cause you're spoiling things. Bye-bye!"

And he carried Slocum upstairs. On the landing Robin was holding a door open. Monty carried him across the threshold, dumped him on a bed and then held him down. He glimpsed Robin, and behind her, Gully coming into the room. Then Robin was bending over him, holding a glass of whiskey.

"Come on, honey," she crooned, "drink. You'll feel better. You'll calm down."

He tried to swing at the glass, but Robin got it out of the way in time.

"What are you doing that for, baby? It's good whiskey!"

"Who the hell wants whiskey?" John raged, struggling under the grinning Monty.

"But it's good for you! Drink. Come on. Drink."

"Gimme that!" Monty seized the tumbler. He signaled to Gully. Gully nodded and grabbed John's arms. Monty set his knee on Slocum's chest and then, with one huge hand he gripped Slocum's head. With the other he brought the drink forward.

"You heard the little lady. She said it's good for you. So, you gonna drink."

The glass was pushed against his mouth. The stink was closer now, overpowering, rancid, foul, bringing up vomit. He retched and as his mouth opened, the glass tilted and the liquor was poured in. He choked and gagged and swallowed and the whiskey flamed down his throat.

Gully let go. Monty let go.

"That ought to calm you down," Gully said. "You just had a mickey finn."

Slocum stared. He saw Monty laughing and Robin looking nervous and uneasy. Gully smiling. He couldn't smell the stink of death anymore. Just himself. His own defeat. His own victimization, which wasn't death, just a chill emptiness of living, of being alive and being betrayed.

He bobbed up and down as the springs of the bed bounced. A clown. A puppet on undiscoverable strings. Then suddenly he pitched forward. He would have hit the brass bed rail if Monty hadn't caught him.

Gently, lovingly, as if he was a pet, Monty laid him down on the bed. Robin and Gully gazed at Slocum.

Slowly the faces, furniture, and room blurred as the drug took effect. A hard bright starburst of light flared in his face and was gone.

And then he knew no more.

11

The Vanner brothers, in the pale radiance of the moon, came riding down the slope. In the ghostly light they rode close together, bunched and in the wan silveriness they seemed the great gallop of a single nocturnal beast.

Chris and Billy were muffled in bearskin coats and Job wore a buffalo hide. The air was chill and in the piñon and juniper, small dark night hunters scurried out of their way, and cried.

Below them, partly in shadow, partly in the spectral light, a ranch house, outbuildings and corrals stood. No lights shone. Inside the house there was measured breathing and a clock ticking off the blind darkness.

The Vanner brothers leveled out, rode rapidly up to a fence, reined in and dismounted. Abruptly, a dog began to furiously bark.

In a bedroom of the house, Sam Bent sat up. He looked at the window through which moonlight was streaming. Then he reached over and shook the bulky figure lying beside him.

"Janie! Janie!"

"What?"

"Listen," Sam said. "The dog. Listen."

The bedsprings creaked and Mrs. Bent sat up.

"Something's out there. In the yard." He threw the covers off and swung out of bed. His nightgown caught under his thighs. He turned to pull it loose. At that moment the moonlight disappeared and shadows fell across the bed.

"What. . . ." Sam got out and started to jerk around.

A turmoil of great, shapeless shadows surged up and across the window. Sam stared for an instant, paralyzed, his heart clenched with terror. What the hell was coming out of the night? What? Then: the rifle! It flashed through his mind. The goddamn rifle! He sprang up, but the window crashed inwards and, as the glass shattered, the shadows leaped into the room.

Mrs. Bent screamed.

"Shut!" one of the shadows murderously said.

"Vanner!" Sam said. "Chris Vanner!"

He could see them now. Three of them, looming about him, moonlight on their faces and gleaming on their guns.

"I wanna know something."

Slowly, trembling now, Sam sat on the bed. His wife clung to him.

"You hear me?" It was Chris and the voice was getting higher, shriller. "I wanna know something!"

"Wha . . . what?"

"They can't get no jury in town. But they ain't let Lee go. Two weeks already. Two weeks! Why they ain't letting him go?"

Sam worked his throat. He wanted to get the words out. But something cold and sweating and sickening was in the way. Job moved up to him and swung. The slap knocked him back against his wife and the words broke loose.

"Sheriff Dunn! He . . . he's collecting a jury outside of town. Picking them up. Anybody passing through. Holding them. Nobody in town, I swear it! God's honest truth! Nobody in town'll serve. Only strangers. Tramps. Scum. He . . . he's picking them up. . . ."

"How many he got?"

"Seven, I think. Maybe eight?"

"When?"

90

He turned his head. That was Job.

"What?"

"When they gonna try Lee? When?"

"Five . . . six weeks. When . . . when the judge comes back."

The words stopped. He stared at the three of them. Only their eyes and faces were separate. Their bodies seemed one. Eyes palely glowing in the moonlight like lanterns hung far away. Yet they were not lanterns. They were devil's eyes, fiend's eyes . . . the glare of killers.

Terror surged back.

"Listen," he said. "It ain't my fault. It ain't none of our fault. We . . . we would have gone on that jury and . . . and voted him innocent. Only that Damien. *He* would have killed us. He said it. I swear! We did what we could. It ain't our fault. It ain't . . . !"

In the small bedroom the gun was like a lightning flash. And then there was an explosion of thunder.

The bullet smashed into Sam Bent's head, slamming him back across his wife's legs. The bedsprings bounced, and as Sam bobbed up and down upon her, Mrs. Bent stared. Her mouth was open, but she could make no sound. All of her had failed, leaving shock behind.

Blood was spreading across Sam's nightshirt and onto the coverlet.

"Tell 'em, missus," Chris shrilled, the powder smoke curling from his gun, making him dimmer, as if he was receding. "Tell 'em! That's what'll happen to all of 'em if that sheriff don't stop trying to get a jury. One at a time, it'll happen. You tell 'em. You hear, missus? You tell 'em!"

Chris turned and the light disappeared from the room as he plunged through the broken window. Job and Billy followed and when they were gone, the moon was streaming in again and Mrs. Bent could see the dark spread of blood. Once more the dog began to bark.

And, Mrs. Bent, feeling the heavy weight across her knees, screamed. And screamed and screamed.

12

The sunlight sliced through the boarded up windows as thin as knifeblades.

In the bed under the covers were two huddled figures. When the light reached the pillows, Slocum was the first to sit up.

"God!" he said and grabbed his head. It was breaking loose and falling off. He felt it crack and begin to shatter as though it was a piece of statuary.

"God Almighty!" He held it tightly, but everything else was going, an avalanche of his entire being, sliding, plunging against the backs of his eyes.

"Jesus! God! Jesus!"

Beside him, something stirred. He could not see

too well. A blur of something, a darkish stain, of what? Hair?

"Good morning, honey!"

He shook his head. Even the words hurt.

"What's the matter? Don't you recognize me? Robin!"

He blinked his eyes. Robin? A call. A trill. A bird. Orange breasted. Breasted. Robin!

"A mickey!" Slocum yelled and grabbed at her. "You slipped me a mickey!"

"Ah, honey, I'm sorry." The stain was hair, and eyes and mouth. "But I couldn't help it. Orders. So you wouldn't make more trouble."

She pushed against him. He felt her. Naked. He grabbed the covers, flung them back and sprang out of bed. He staggered, seized a chair, steadied himself and startled, saw that he was raw naked, too.

"I undressed you, Slocum."

Enraged, he got up, went to the door, seized the knob and pulled. He rattled the knob. Then he let go of it and banged on the wooden door.

"Ah, come on," Robin sat up. "Be good. Be nice."

Her arms lay on the covers and her breasts were exposed, round, dark-nippled, soft. She was as public as himself, accessible to any insult or humiliation. But, there was no shame, no outrage, no private ego.

"You come on here, honey," she gently said. "Hold Robin. Come on. It's better than banging and kicking the door. Hold Robin."

93

Abruptly he rushed to the bed. He dropped to his knees beside it. Her arms reached for his shoulders.

"Help me get out of here," he said slowly.

"Come into bed, John."

"You don't understand. What it means." She was drawing him closer.

"It's a lousy life, John. I know it. A lousy, stinking life. It's fixed up for losers. Believe me. It's patched up for them. So come on, come to bed."

She bent forward and kissed his cheek. Then, gently, she pressed his head down.

Downstairs, in the gray, dusty morning light, Gully was sorting out keys. In a few minutes, he'd ascend, knock, unlock the doors and call out:

"Breakfast, ladies and gents. Breakfast!"

He worked quietly. Unhurriedly. In a gray peace. Like stone.

13

Sam Bent, covered with a tarp and dead as butcher-shop beef, shuddered and shook as the flatbed wagon rattled down the rutted street.

Coxey, who owned the General Mercantile Store, was leading the horse, and around him swirled an angry crowd.

Sam Bent was riding in southwestern pomp. The faint but pungent smell of horse manure clung to this weathered caisson.

Ranchers and merchants, the citizens of Blindman, escorted the deceased. Their faces red and
sweating, their eyes piggish with fury, they shook
their fists and shouted:

"Run 'em out!"

"Get them bastards out of town!"

"Kick 'em out! Beat 'em out!"

"Shoot their asses off till they're out of here!"

Down the street with horse, wagon and bobbing
corpse, they spilled like a muddy torrent. They saw
the window at the sheriff's office shoot up. Pop
stuck his head out and stared. At the jail window, a
startled Lee Vanner appeared. Pop pulled back and
a moment later he was in the window again, holding a shotgun in his hands.

Breakfast was in full swing at the Union Saloon.
Ham and eggs. Enchiladas, tortillas, frijoles, dome-
shaped Spanish bread, steaming coffee, all brought
in swift succession by Gully.

Sam Ely, Buck, Tex, Goldtooth and Monty were
gorging themselves. Slocum sat with them, brood-
ing over a mug of coffee. Damien was near the
doors, as usual, sipping his coffee, holding his
weapon.

None of the girls were down yet.

"What the hell!" Monty suddenly said and
slammed down his mug. He turned his huge head.
Damien was already standing watchfully at the
doors.

Gully halted, put down a bowl of frijoles and also listened.

Then all of them heard it. The shouting.

Damien put his coffee on his chair and stepped outside. One by one the jurors rose, crumbs on their shirts, bits of food clinging to their lips. One by one they registered it, the sound of threat taking shape outside. Gully turned and went to the bar for his gun.

The crowd had reached the saloon. Outside, on the portal, Damien was standing with his shotgun cradled in his arms, gazing with a faint, puzzled wonder at them as though anyone else's fury always left him mildly surprised.

The jurors were crowding in the doorway behind him, and then Gully pushed through and was alongside Damien, armed.

"Bent! That's Sam Bent!" Coxey screamed, pointing to the wagon. "Under that tarp!" He moved toward the portal, a gaunt man, rage making him look as if his face had been axed. "You satisfied now?"

"The Vanner brothers!" It was Judson from the livery stable. It was his wagon, his horse. "The Vanners! They done it!"

A startled movement went through the jurors, a kind of group lurch and jerk. Surprised looks were shot at each other. Who? The Vanner brothers. *Brothers?*

Up on the gallery above the portal some of the girls appeared, holding wrappers tightly about themselves. They leaned over the balustrade, their hair wild, their eyes alarmed.

"They murdered him!" Coxey shouted. "Shot him down in his own bed!"

"As a warning!" McAllistair, a rancher, cried. "Not to hold a trial. Not to convict Lee!"

"Jesus," whispered Buck, stunned, "how many Vanners is there?"

"So?" Damien was immovable.

"So, out!" Coxey shook his fist at them. "Get 'em out! Them tramps! That goddamn flea-bitten jury. Get 'em all out of here!"

"Or, by God, we'll burn down your lousy saloon!"

The crowd surged forward, shouting: "Out! Run 'em out of town!"

Damien uncradled the shotgun, aimed toward heaven and fired. The weapon roared and the crowd became silent.

"I've got another load," he patted the gun, "who wants it?"

For a moment the crowd choked on its own rage. Then McAllistair broke loose and shouted: "Listen, you scum, convict him, then the Vanners'll kill us all. One by one. Them dumb bastard jurors *included*! They promised it. The three of them up in them mountains like the Apocalypse, swearing to take vengeance. You know it as good as us!"

Robin was on the gallery now. She leaned over, cupped her lips and called down:

97

"Go on out and bury him, will you? Sam is starting to stink!"

"Sam's been stinking for years!" Lola cried.

The girls laughed. Now the morning was becoming familiar.

"You stink!" Coxey screamed at them. "You all stink!" He jerked back to Damien. "You get them jurors out of town!"

Damien, his face looking somehow thinner, as if such moments as these purified it, redeemed him spiritually, broke open the shotgun, ejected the spent shell and slipped another in its place. Then he clicked the gun shut.

"First who trespasses on my property," he said with a solemn joy, "gets both barrels and joins Sam Bent."

Lee Vanner yelled shrilly from the jail window:

"The hell with them! Bust me out, you goddamn fools! Don't bother none with them. Bust *me* out!"

"That's right," Judson swung about, "he's right! Bust him out and we're all off the hook! Get rid of *him*! Let him go!"

"Damnit, that's what we've got to do!"

"Get *him* out of here!"

"That's what you got to do!" Lee Vanner caught the sudden, brand-new excitement of the crowd. He made frantic love to it. "Me! You dumb bastards! Me! I'm the important one! Bust me out of here!"

And the crowd turned, wheeling like a huge and clumsy flock of crows, and swarmed toward the jail, crying:

"Vanner! Lee Vanner! Lee Vanner!"

Another shotgun roared. The crowd stopped.

In the window of the sheriff's office was Pop, his weapon still raised. One blast and he'd brought down the entire flock.

On the gallery, the girls laughed.

"Now, gents," Damien's voice was gentle, brotherly, "you're caught between two fires. That ain't good business."

Slowly, brokenly, the crowd turned. Damien was descending to the street, his shotgun leveled, smiling, approaching like a friendly, cheery demon. Behind him, under the portal, the jurors were still bunched, silent, wide-eyed. Nearby waited Gully, fixed silently to his gun.

"So," Damien was near to singing, "all you brave fellows go on home. I can hear your wives calling. Your children. And your beef and cash registers and your merchandise. Your beans, your flour and your fodder, all calling, begging you to come on home."

He halted, the twin barrels of his shotgun probing curiously at Coxey's belly. They gently touched the man's shirt, tapped it, circled between belt and string tie.

"Goddamn you!" It was Lee Vanner. "You sons-of-bitch idiots! Get me out! Me! Me!"

But the crowd remained unresponsive, motionless, all watching the beady eyes of Damien's gun.

"So," Damien continued, his voice soft and intimate, "I'm going to count to three. That's all I

99

know. Can't count no more. Fact is, never needed to. Anyway, going to count and then one of you is going to get a load of buckshot in the guts. For inciting to riot." His face flashed with a warm gleam. "One."

"You . . . you'll regret this." Coxey was sweating.

"Never regretted nothing," Damien shrugged. "Two."

"Bastard!" Coxey spun on his heel, grabbed at the horse's bridle and pulled. The wagon groaned and creaked and bumped forward. Under the tarp, Sam Bent's corpse shook. The wagon rattled down the road. The crowd fell apart. Ragged, broken now, the crowd strung out, following.

The girls cried:

"Sam's getting high!"

"We can smell him up here!"

Damien turned and looked up at them. The girls fled out of sight. Then, leisurely, he strolled back to the portal. At the bottom step he halted and smiled at the jurors.

"Show's over, gents," he said. "Meanwhile, breakfast is getting cold."

And he herded them back inside.

At the table, they barely touched the food. They gazed at the disarray of plenty. The ham and eggs. The frijoles. The coffee. And they brooded.

Damien was beside the doors again. Gully was behind the bar.

Beans, when they did touch them, were cold. Eggs were chilled. The coffee was bitter.

Then, low, whispering, Goldtooth said, "You heard 'em. Good as I did. Vanner brothers. Three of 'em!"

"In the mountains," Buck said.

"Like the Apocalypse. To take vengeance!"

"On us, too." Goldtooth nudged Sam Ely's arm. "Including us, too."

"We been conned. Had," Sam hollowly said. "If we convict, we're dead men."

Slocum watched. Listened. Yet he heard them as though they were far away, their voices reaching him disembodied but clear.

"Conned?" Goldtooth fumed. "We been suckered! Bamboozled! Diddled!"

"This country's full of Vanners, and all with guns!"

Sam Ely nodded, his narrow cardsharp's eyes squinting. He smiled vaguely at Buck. Then he looked at Monty who sat mountainously, staring into some distance as if he'd come upon a sudden, brand-new range in the sky.

Then, Sam Ely smiled. He understood it all. It *was* all new. A brand-new unexpected geography.

"Well, in that case," he solemnly murmured, "we just don't convict."

"What?"

The others looked at him. Even Monty turned away from his vision.

101

"We vote him innocent," Sam said, the vague smile now beatific, transformed, "them Vanners then got nothing against us. Innocent as a lamb let him go forth. We oblige the Vanner family in their need."

For a moment more they gazed at Sam. And then, as if the beatific smile was like a gentle spring zephyr, it touched them all. It ruffled each one's soul, lifted each man's spirits. That is, all except Slocum's.

As Sam's smile spread, Slocum's face went dark.

"Meantime," Sam's voice was blessing them, "we can go on collecting a dollar a day and having a son of a bitch of a time!"

"Shit!" Slocum said.

They stared, startled, while he grasped and struggled with a tangle of things. Finally:

"You . . . you mean . . . you deciding the case *now*? You voting him innocent *now*?"

His outrage was still enormous. It roared through him faster than his blood.

Sam nodded. The others nodded.

"Goddamnit!" Slocum gripped the table edge to hold himself down. "You mean it's all going to be for nothing? Six weeks for nothing? It ain't even going to be worth it? It's all settled? Now? And I've got to be hooked, chained, nailed into this damn place for nothing?"

"We're getting off the hook, son," Sam Ely apostolically said.

"Ah shit!" Slocum said again, his blood catching

102

up to his rage now. "You're out of your minds! I ain't sticking around to play out a lousy, fixed, stacked game! I ain't even performing a public duty! It's a goddamn circus! I'm going to see the sheriff! I'm going to talk. And, I'm getting out of here! I'm. . . . "

The mountain dropped. Monty gripped his arm. Slocum could feel the granite, the iron in it.

"Now lookee here," Monty said, and showed his teeth through the brush of his beard. It was like abruptly coming upon a burned and blasted stand of great trees, a place of fire and lightning and destruction.

"Don't you spoil our good time. Like Sam says, don't you go messing up our luck. Open your yap and I'll break your neck. Jesus, I'll sure bust your spine!"

Monty's smile broadened. And Slocum saw farther and farther into that charred and devastated world.

And the others only saw heaven.

14

Slocum staggered, then righted himself and downed still another drink. He leaned against the bar. He turned and glared.

Christy was banging away at the piano and the legs of the girls were kicking up and then pounding the floor. Billows of skirts and petticoats surged as they danced in a jagged chorus line, their arms across one another's shoulders.

The jurors, scattered about the room, whistled and clapped and the noise and the music and the girls kicking up small explosions of underthings was like a kind of half-blind pandemonium.

Slocum swayed, his being fixed to a drunken gaze that was supposed to see nothing but the whiskey-yellow light of heaven. His hands held on to the bar. His hair was damp. His tall figure swayed like the slow pulse of the sea.

The music galloped and smashed to its end. The girls buried it with squeals. More whistles. More clapping. Then Monty was lumbering across the floor, seizing a girl in each arm and hugging them.

"Lordy! Lordy!" he boomed. "Beauties! Warm and living beauties! Juicy berries! And there I was hunting in the hills and the best fresh meat was all the time right down here!"

Again the massive squeeze, the giant embrace.

"Oh, beauties! Yessir! Wild melons juicy in my arms! I'm gonna bust! Lordy! I sure love the law! The grandest thing in this here republic!"

There were cheers and laughter.

"To Mr. Damien!" Goldtooth sprang to his feet and raised a tumbler to the man smiling at the doors. "Them bastards would have busted up a good thing. But Mr. Damien, he come like the cavalry!"

With his free hand he cupped his mouth.

"Tara! Tara!" he bugled. "Charge! And he chased them all away! To Mr. Damien!"

Glasses rose to the toast. Whiskey was downed. Only Slocum didn't drink. Instead he stared into his glass for a moment. Then he slammed it down.

"He's getting obstreperous again," Sam Ely murmured, and solemnly, drunk, he moved to the bar.

"Now, don't be gloomy, son," he said to Slocum, relishing his own kindness. He laid a card on the bar.

"The deuce! I look at it, son, and I think: 'Life is real! Life is earnest! And the grave is not the goal!' "

Slocum stared at the deuce. Life and death, lying there, soiled and yellowish, near a ring of wetness on the bar.

"The deuce? Thought it was for the Bible?" Slocum's voice was abrupt. "In two parts. Old and New Testaments."

Sam waved his arm.

"Cards is flexible, son. Made to fit the moment." Sam Ely smiled broadly.

"Come on, boy, dance! Sing! Enjoy! 'Tell me not in mournful numbers life is but an empty dream. . . . ' "

"It sure ain't," Slocum said, and turned sharply. He saw Robin beside the piano.

"Shove your deuce," he said, and long-legged, gangling, like a great bird awkward on the ground, he strode across the floor. He grabbed hold of Robin.

"Hey!" she exclaimed.

105

A half-dozen jurors rose in alarm. What the hell? He was going to make trouble? Out of the corner of his eye, Slocum saw Monty let go of his girls and quietly pick up a bottle.

"Let's go!" Slocum barked.

"What?"

"Upstairs. To your room." He pulled Robin toward him.

"What for?"

"What do you mean 'what for'? What do you think?"

He waited a fraction of a moment, waited until he saw the surprise coming into her eyes. Then he spun around.

"And what the hell you looking at?" he shouted at the others. "You enjoy yourselves one way. Me another!"

Monty guffawed and put the bottle down. Grins of relief began to break out.

"Ah, Slocum honey," Robin protested. "It's kind of early."

There was a raucous shout and Christy banged one single, twanging, jangling chord on the piano.

"Tara!" Goldtooth trumpeted. "Tara! Charge!"

"Well, you coming upstairs?"

Robin was unsure. She sent a glance toward Damien. Damien smiled and nodded.

"Well," and Robin shrugged, "you're the boss."

A tiny fire blazed up inside of Slocum. Shut it down, he told himself in panic. Shut it down! Don't show it! Grab her! Pull her! Start moving upstairs!

"Come on, damnit!" He yanked, dragging Robin across the room.

"Life is real!" Sam Ely cheered. "And sure earnest!"

"Go to it, son," Goldtooth cackled, "go to it, boy!"

"Slow down, Slocum," Robin was laughing now, "slow down!"

They were climbing the stairs, Slocum pulling her, the piano resoundingly thumping their progress:

" 'Here comes the bride!

Here comes the bride!' "

When they reached the landing, Slocum dragged her into the room.

Sam Ely laid down a card on the bar.

"The deuce," he intoned, "yessir, when I see the deuce, I think on Robin and John!"

"Beauties," Monty boomed, scooping up a girl in each arm, "beauties! Three cheers for the Land of the Free!"

Slocum shut the door and leaned against it. He could still hear the piano downstairs, but it was a sound he had already left far behind.

"You sure are a sudden man," Robin was turning up the lamp, "and sure commanding!"

She laughed, faced the mirror and began to loosen her hair. He looked hard at her, just once, the arms raised pulling pins, the rosy shine of her face. A glow, he abruptly realized, was always there.

"Going to buy her something some day," he told himself, and with that he went for the window. He gripped the sash and pulled.

"Hey!"

The goddamn catch was shut. Slocum released it and then the window shot up with a rasp.

"What are you doing?" Her hair was piled upon her shoulders now. She came toward Slocum. "You're going to let in drafts, John. Through those slats."

"Get back," Slocum said. "Get the hell out of my way." He raised his booted leg and smashed it into the nailed boards.

"John!" She ran at him.

"I said get the hell away from me!" He shoved her aside and kicked viciously at the boards again. One slat screeched free.

"What are you trying to do?"

"Get out of here, that's what!" And once more he kicked. The board ripped completely away from the window.

For a moment, Robin was shocked and terrified.

"John, they'll beat me to pieces!"

But he was now smashing his feet against another board. She turned, raced for the door, opened it and fled, shouting:

"Damien! Damien!"

He heard her shouting as he flung himself at the remaining boards. His shoulders smashed into them. They cracked, splintered and ripped loose and Slocum went sprawling through the window, tumbling head first onto the gallery above the portal.

The first thing he did when he sprang up was to swallow the chill night air. Freedom! It went through him like a lightning flash, through his entire body. A galvanic burst of energy. Then he raced to the gallery rail, looked down and saw a saddled horse hitched to a post across the street.

God! A man breaks for freedom and miracles and luck are everywhere! He swung a leg over the rail. Jump!

At that moment Damien appeared. He came racing out of the saloon, looking upwards, the shotgun ready in his hands.

And instantly, Slocum jumped. Dropped knees first. He landed as hard as he could upon Damien. Like a felled tree, Damien went down, the shotgun skittering across the rutted ground.

Slocum leaped up, lunged at it, grabbed it by the barrels and turned and swung. Damien was beginning to rise when the gunstock caught him alongside the head. He was unconscious before he hit the ground again.

John was running for the horse now. He could hear Gully and the jurors and the girls spilling out of the saloon. He got the hitch loose and jumped into the saddle. He kicked the animal and the horse lurched and then started to gallop. Slocum raised the shotgun and aimed it murderously at the small crowd before the saloon. Everyone froze, watching the barrels. And Slocum galloped away.

15

The undertaking parlor faced the street and inside, Sam Bent lay in a box that rested upon four stools.

Men, dressed in black, stood about in silence while their women, like weathered carvings, were seated along one wall. All were watching the sheriff as he stood beside the box, paying his last respects.

Dunn, holding his hat in his hands, was wishing it was a gun. Any one of those bastards behind him would like to shoot him in the back. Dump *him* into that box, shove him underground.

He, the law, threatened their lives. The carrying out of justice was a menace, but it had to be in this world. It had to exist. He thought of Lee Vanner and he felt sick with hate and rage.

"Sheriff." It was Coxey. He was standing opposite Dunn now, between him and the plate-glass window.

"Yeah?"

The man's face was grim, a narrow slice of his own hate.

"It's your fault, you know that, don't you?"

"My fault?"

"That's right."

He heard a whispering shuffle of feet as if they were crowding up behind him, crowding him out of some darkness.

110

"Sam's lying there on account of you."

"Bastard," he breathed slowly, "you bastard!"

"He'd be walking the earth today, but for you."

Dunn placed his hands and his hat on the box and leaned forward, glaring.

"Listen, you damn fool, I got the law to uphold."

"The law!" Coxey spat it. "You're supposed to keep us alive! Us! And all you've done. . . ."

And suddenly, through the plate-glass window they saw a horse and rider galloping by. They plunged across the line of vision like some demonic, enormous, monstrous apparition.

"What the hell!" the sheriff exclaimed and charged for the door. When he reached it, Coxey grabbed his arm.

"Haven't you any respect, either?"

"Get the hell away, you jackass fool!"

And the sheriff shoved. Coxey went staggering back against the coffin. As the box crashed to the floor, Dunn was outside and running like a madman toward the saloon.

16

Pale and thin, a grayish-blue light was upon the world. The sagebrush plain, outflung and vast, lay as if it had just died, and in the distance the mountains, chilled and slate-colored, huddled in the predawn air.

Between his knees, the horse heaved and labored.

He's going to drop soon, Slocum thought. He's going to cave in. But he had to get through this bleached world, this sage graveyard, across this gritty universe, away from the sharp, bony smell of dry juniper and pine.

He jerked on the reins. The horse came up in a cloud of sand, with front hooves flailing, kicking about it in panic.

Where the hell was he? He gripped the shotgun in one hand and rose in the stirrups. Where had he ridden in the dark? And where was the river? Goddamnit, which way?

He twisted in the saddle, and he saw it. The edge of light behind the mountains, a narrow silvery gleam at their crests, and he knew what was east. He wrenched the horse's head around.

"Move! Move!"

Slocum kicked the horse south.

So was Sheriff John Dunn riding south. But he'd been heading that way for hours, as if the man he was trailing would only press on in one direction. This much of another man's desperate passion the sheriff comprehended, and stolidly he rode, pursuing it.

The sun had risen, spilling across the western flanks of the mountains and on to the sagebrush plains below. Dunn sweated and cursed. Riding this country in the white, dazzling light of day when the Vanners could be anywhere! Not only was he trailing a dumb beast, but a damn fool, too!

Low, rolling piñon hills were ahead of him. Overhead, a blue sky, in which turkey buzzards circled and soared. He came up the side of a piñon hill like a tiny boat sailing upon a great sea.

On the crest of the hill, he reined in. He could see fifty miles to the Jemez Mountains. A bluish haze rested on their tops, but at their feet spreading toward him, the sagebrush was sharp and clear.

He sat absolutely still, watching. On this gigantic plain, continuous movement, movement in a long enough arc could be seen. He turned his head imperceptibly and then he stopped.

Movement. A far horseman.

"Son of a bitch," he muttered, "in broad daylight across this plain!"

17

At first Slocum didn't notice it. He rode, crouched over his horse with only one thought in his head. Distance! Get distance!

The sand and the sage had gently been rising on either side of him, like two unobtrusive, outstretched arms. He plunged into and between them and it was not until he realized that he could no longer see the enormous distances, that he pulled up short. He had ridden into an arroyo.

The walls were already head high. Layers of a reddish clay streaked their sides. Wind and rain and old floods had weirdly carved them, but here and

there on the arid, desiccated walls, clumps of wild
yellow zinnias still clung.

"Out of here!" Slocum said, alarmed. He yanked
on the reins to pull the horse around. At that moment he caught sight of lush, vivid green grass up
ahead. Water!

He pulled the horse front again and galloped
deeper into the arroyo. The walls were some twenty
feet high when the thread of water glittered in the
sun. A trickle. But enough.

He leaped off the saddle, dropped to his knees,
buried his face in the water and drank. His horse
joined him, mouth and muzzle sucking up the wet.

After a while, Slocum leaned back. He still held
the shotgun. He put it on the ground, took off his
hat and scooping up water, drenched his head and
face.

It was like coming alive again, like being resur-
rected, springing back to life like whipping steel.
Vigorous, cold and strong and active and twanging
with hope.

"All right. You're cooled off proper."

It was sound, not meaning, that triggered him.
A voice, the first thrust of it, that was all. The
words went piling up, unlistened to as Slocum spun
and dove for the gun.

"Touch it and I'll blow your brains out."

This time the words had meaning. They arranged
themselves like set stones. Slocum sat back and
looked up.

Above him, on the arroyo wall, still on his horse,

his weapon unwavering in his hand, was the sheriff. Against the blue sky, horse and rider loomed dark, their edges, though, glowing with a pale, silvery light. Another sun rising!

"Get your hands further away from that shotgun!"

Slocum drew his fingers back.

"Now stand up, slow and easy, like you're just enjoying the morning air."

He came up slowly, as the sheriff suggested, and in that moment, everything seemed suddenly unreal. And the things around him, the arroyo, the glitter of the stream, even the shining barrel of the shotgun, all strange.

"Get your horse."

Slocum turned, and groped for the animal's reins. Something was missing.

"Get on it and come on up here."

"Shit!" He spun around facing the sheriff. "Like hell I will! No!"

The hammer clicked back sharp and clear.

"You can still go on a jury with a bullet in your leg."

But Slocum was whole now. Insight had fused him complete.

"Jury? What jury? You ain't got no jury! All you've got is a stacked deck. Christ! You don't even need a jury. They've already made their verdict. They can mail it to you! Or leave you an affidavit!"

"I've got no time to argue," Dunn tensely said. "Them Vanners could be anywhere."

John began screaming.

"Didn't you hear me? They've already *made* their verdict. Innocent! Not guilty, on account of being afraid! They've already agreed. They're getting off the hook. They ain't going to judge anybody at all!"

"That why you lit out?"

"You're goddamn right, that's why! And I ain't going back! Not to something where it don't make any difference if I'm there or not!"

"Ah, but it will make a difference, sonny," the sheriff harshly said, "and you are going back."

Suddenly Dunn kicked his horse. The animal, astonished, plunged forward. Horse and rider came down the bank of the arroyo with sand geysering about them. Slocum saw his own horse rear in alarm and in that sand-blurred moment he dived for his gun. He got his hands on it. He straightened up and then his horse, still rearing, slammed up against him. He tried to recover, tried to swing so that he'd be facing the sheriff, but he went lurching to his knees and his finger pulled the trigger.

In the walled arroyo, the shotgun roared. The sound rushed in great explosive waves against the banks, then back at him, then again at the banks, then up at the sky and spreading, reached for limitless space, for vastness to free itself.

As it echoed and ricocheted, Dunn leaped at him. They hit the ground together. Into the stream they rolled, their arms wildly flailing, water scattering from them like hundreds of gleaming knives.

The gun, Slocum thought frantically. What hap-

116

pened to the goddamn gun? Then he realized the sheriff didn't have a weapon either. What the hell happened to the guns?

The sheriff used his fists like clubs. Flesh and water slammed at him. Then he was free. He sat up, hip-deep in water, and saw the sheriff scrambling, scooping up his pistol and then whirling around furiously, shouting.

"Get up, you bastard! Get on that horse! They could have heard that shot in Denver! Get on that horse!"

"You go to hell."

"You hear me?"

"I ain't getting on no horse!"

Slocum soaking in the stream, the cold making him sound hysterical, cursed and screamed obscenities at the sheriff. His hands were in the water, each one clutched murderously around a rock.

"You stupid idiot!"

Dunn ran into the water, seized Slocum by the shirtfront and started dragging him out. Slocum let go of the rocks. He clutched at the sheriff's hands as he was twisted and pulled and hauled to dry grass. When Dunn yanked him to his feet, he also brought the pistol up.

"It's a spitting distance away from firing," Dunn's voice was trembling, "get on that horse if you want to live!"

"You're goddamn right I want to live!" Dripping, his hair pasted to his forehead, Slocum grabbed at the pommel. "But in my own way, mister. In my own way!"

And he sprang on the horse, kicked it and charged full tilt at the sheriff.

"You devil!" The sheriff leaped clear and Slocum went thundering past. Dunn raised his gun. Then, he jerked his hand down.

"Denver?" He muttered aloud. "They'd hear it in Chicago!"

A moment later he was on his own horse and pounding after Slocum, both of them now, riding deeper into the arroyo.

After a while the arroyo banks were getting steeper and the stream wider and besides lush green grass, there were clumps of willows now. Through its twists and turns, the two riders galloped, kicking up spurts of water, of mud, pebbles and sand.

Each time he turned in the saddle, Slocum saw the sheriff closer. A fresher horse, damnit! And under him a laboring, blowing plug! Closer all the time, until, pounding down a straight stretch, Slocum turned and there was the sheriff almost on top of him.

"Move! Move!" he screamed at the animal under him, punching it in the head and kicking its flanks. "Move!"

The horse did spurt, or lurch, or stagger or do something, but only for a second. Then it seemed to fall backwards and the sheriff was alongside, reaching out, grabbing Slocum and jerking him.

Slocum came off the horse as if he'd hit an invisible tree. His legs gyrated wildly for an instant, and then he slammed into the ground, sending up a midget hurricane of water and sand.

When he stopped rolling and spinning and tried to spring up, it was too late. Dunn had jumped him, flinging him down again, straddling him, one big meaty hand pressing him into the mud and water, the other shoving a gun barrel at his eyes.

"I've had enough of you!" Dunn was livid with rage. "You hear me? Enough!"

"It's mutual," Slocum cried, swallowing water as he struggled in the stream. "It's goddamn mutual!"

"All of you! Every single one of you! All you've got in your heads is your own way! Your own stinking little interests!"

He shook Slocum and water flooded his nose and eyes. Slocum was coughing now.

"The hell with what's right or wrong! The hell with justice!"

And he stepped back and hauled Slocum to his feet. Water still ran down his face and clothes. The sheriff still gripped him, still waved the gun in his eyes, still went on with his tirade.

"Maybe it's a waste of time to get justice. Maybe I ought to shoot you, here and now! And then the whole scabby lot! Bums and ranchers! Drifters and merchants! Rid the earth of all of you! Feed your face! Feed your pockets! That's all you can think on! Damnit," shaking Slocum with uncon-

119

trollable fury. "I should have killed that Lee Vanner when he was stark-naked in the Rio Grande! But no! No! I wanted justice! I wanted it right and fair! I ought to blow your heads off! All of you! I. . . ."

And suddenly, Dunn halted. His eyes blazed and then narrowed. He could see Slocum wasn't listening! He could see Slocum staring, yes, but not at him. Past him. Beyond him.

"Look at me, damnit!" and he shook him violently, "look at me when I'm talking!"

"Company." Slocum said.

"What?"

"Back there. Coming up the arroyo."

Dunn swung around and for an instant he seemed to see nothing. Then they both heard it. Horses.

And abruptly, out of the willow clumps far down the arroyo, they appeared. Three riders. Crouched over their mounts, splashing silvery splinters of water as they galloped on.

"That's them!" the sheriff exploded. "The Vanners!"

He started running toward the horses, pulling Slocum with him.

"Get going!"

"No!" Slocum said and stopped dead. He planted his feet stubbornly against the ground. "Go where? Back to town?"

"Listen, you dumb ox!"

"I told you! No! I ain't being no part of any lying game!"

120

"You want to live?"

" 'Course I do!"

"Then get the hell out of here!"

"I've got nothing against them," Slocum gestured at the galloping riders.

Dunn stared at him. Then he nodded emphatically.

"You want to die? All right, then! I've had enough! Stay here!"

And the sheriff let go of him, raced to his horse and Slocum watched him swing up in the saddle, spur the animal and pound away.

For a moment, Slocum watched him. One going. He turned. Three coming. They were coming fast now. He could hear them. They were shouting and whooping. He had a moment of uncertainty. They were coming like it was a drunken Saturday night. Like they were on a spree. Like they were on a wild time. Maybe he should have. . . .

Then a gun exploded. He heard it coming up the arroyo at him, and with a sudden clutching of astonishment Slocum saw the bullet smack the ground not five yards away.

What the hell! What were they doing? Shooting just because he was alive?

He felt a panic, an alarm so great that he stood there, rooted. They didn't know him from Adam, and the moment they saw him, they were blasting away. What the hell kind of madmen were around here?

Again the gun roared. Slocum jerked around,

ran for his horse and galloped crazily after the sheriff.

18

The first one to come out of the arroyo was Sheriff Dunn. Ahead of him the ground began to rise, lifting toward massive volcanic boulders and huge rock slides.

He pulled up for an instant, and as his horse sidestepped and jerked and reared, he saw Slocum come galloping out of the arroyo. Then he heard the more distant drumming of hooves, like the multileveled reverberation of a single approaching rider.

Dunn gestured at the rock slides ahead.

"Keep going!" he yelled to Slocum, and kicked his horse and galloped on.

Up the sloping ground Slocum came. His horse was stumbling now and patches of gray-white sweat, like a leprosy, had appeared on the animal's neck and rump. Its breath was coming in great harsh rips. But Slocum could hear the riders behind him, their hooves thudding and their yelling. He pushed his horse on.

Among the volcanic boulders and rock slides he drove the horse on, kicking it unmercifully. Steadily the ground rose and then, abruptly, he couldn't see the sheriff anymore. Panic stabbed back and he kicked the horse's sides.

"Come on! Goddamnit, come on!"

The horse labored up and then it was over a ridge of rock and there, ahead of him, was the sheriff, sitting on his blowing horse, staring bitterly at a vast, wide, expanse of sky.

Slocum reined in. Good God! A wide, treeless, rock shelf! To his left were tumbled, gigantic boulders, like piled, enormous ruins of a dead and monumental world. And ahead, nothing. Only the sheriff and an unending blueness, an airiness, a sheer drop.

He clattered across the shelf.

"Where the hell you lead me?" Slocum cried, aghast. "What the hell you think I got? Wings?"

They could both hear the riders below them. Without answering, the sheriff jerked his horse's head around and galloped toward the jumble of great rocks.

"Listen, you bastard!" Slocum shouted and sprinted after Dunn.

The sheriff was swinging off his horse and untangling a canteen of water from the pommel when Slocum reached him.

"Get down!" the sheriff said.

"What?"

"Get off! It's on foot now. And, bring that shotgun!"

"What shotgun?"

Dunn was draping the canteen across his shoulders. He froze for an instant, then turned slowly.

123

"The one you had," he carefully said. "I lost mine. The one you fired. Damien's."

The drumming below them changed. It was clatter now. The Vanners were on the rocks.

"I ain't got it," Slocum said. "It's someplace back there."

"You . . . you left it?" The enormity of it brought a kind of nausea to the sheriff. "Back there? On the ground?"

"You did the same, didn't you?"

"One gun!" The sheriff groaned. "You dumb bastard! One gun, that's all we have. One gun against the whole goddamn world!"

And at that moment, the clatter of the Vanner horses burst upon them. The Vanners came over the ridge.

Billy was in front and as soon as he saw them he started whooping, shrilling, whistling, rising in his saddle like a trick rider, a savage Sioux on the war-path, whacking his horse's rump with a battered hat, his long, uncut hair flying in the wind.

"Come on!" Dunn yelled and raced for the boulders further up the shelf. Slocum jumped, hit the ground, staggered, righted himself and ran as if he was on fire.

"That's it, cousin!" Billy whooped, standing straight up in the stirrups, as if he was feather-light. As if by some magic, he was separate from the horse yet moving as swiftly as the beast below him.

"Run, you jackrabbits! Run!" And he drew his gun and began firing.

Bullets smashed alongside as the sheriff and Slocum scrambled among shattered towers and parapets, scurrying about collapsed mammoth walls, the remains of the earth's violence. And all the while the air exploded and roared with gunshots and echoed with the shrill yelling from Billy.

"Run, cousin! Run!"

Ahead were the huge boulders and a cliff face that seemed to soar forever. Then, suddenly, a split yawned before the sheriff, a crevice, long and narrow, running like a jagged scar up the cliff's wall. Dunn grabbed at Slocum.

"In here!" He pulled. Slocum tripped and fell. He slid in soft sand and the glare of sunlight was gone. He had the sensation of plunging into a dim world, and at the same time, he could smell an old, dry odor of ashes and charred fires. He lurched to his feet and when he turned, there was the sheriff pressed up against one wall, gun in hand, gazing intently out through the crevice opening.

Slocum had the strange feeling that everything that had happened had been ordered, neatly falling into place. Logical. Clicking coolly like an abacus. Only in his own mind had there been confusion and nightmare disorder. It lasted just a second. Then he shook himself.

"Hell, I'm out of my head!" and he moved to the sheriff's side.

The crevice was no more than five feet wide at most, and its walls sloped upwards. But it was high on the shelf and below them, still on their horses,

125

they could see the Vanners. The three of them darted, pranced, shot erratically in and out of the
boulders.

This was the first time Slocum really saw them.
Jesus! What the hell were they? Apaches? Savages?
Naked to the waist, breechcloths, one of them wearing a bearskin vest that kept flapping open on a
bare chest. And the one who'd been standing
straight up? Crazy mad!

Slocum, his eyes widening, watched, as that par-
ticular Vanner abruptly galloped out from behind
the boulders and did a wild cartwheel. He spun
around, his legs splitting and then he landed, full-
seated, back on the saddle. Then he whistled with
a piercing cry.

"Billy." The sheriff said savagely.

Back and forth, Billy went, sitting on the saddle
with his legs on the horse's neck, then riding backward, then swinging down until he was half under
the animal's belly. Riding like a madman, whistling, whooping, shouting all the time.

Slocum had seen Indians—Sioux, Apaches, Plains
Indians—ride like that. As if, although this was
done first, it was the supreme act, the truly terrify-
ing act. The bloody killing that followed was really
unimportant and meant less.

"Hey, cousin!" Billy was shouting as he rode,
"you know us, cousin! Your kinfolk! Your relations!
We ain't gonna hurt no blood of our'n. Hey,
cousin! Hey!"

The other brothers sat on their horses, unmoving.

126

Job watched Billy, faintly grinning. Chris glared up at the cliff's wall.

"It's Billy-boy, cousin! Remember? We've got family bonds!"

"Son of a bitch!" The sheriff gritted and fired.

Slocum ducked as if the roar and reverberations in the narrow crevice would injure him. When the sound rumbled away, he could still see through the dust, Billy. Laughing, riding, stunting crazily below.

He looked away and glanced at Dunn. In the dimness the sheriff's face seemed more fleshless, harder, bonier, as if honed down by hate.

"Hey, cousin, lookit this!" Billy yelled. He brought up both feet on the saddle and stood up. He moved across the shelf like Christ speeding across the waters.

"Listen," Slocum was abruptly angry, "what the hell is he yelling about? Family bonds. Relations."

"Shut up," the sheriff said.

"What do you mean 'shut up'? He's been calling you cousin, ain't he?"

"None of your business."

"None of my business? There's three maniacs down there and I ain't sure how many more is up here! You their kinfolk or not?"

The sheriff spat. "Never in this lifetime."

"But he's been calling. . . ."

"I know what he's been calling. I heard!" Dunn glared at Slocum. "You want to know what I call him?"

"Sure! I'm curious. Before somebody kills me, I'd like to know. I'd consider it a favor!"

For a moment more, the sheriff glared. Then he turned his head back toward the opening. Slocum, following his movement, suddenly grabbed Dunn's arm.

"Billy. The crazy one. He's missing!"

"Up the rocks, probably," the sheriff flatly said. He spun the chamber of his gun, located the spent shell and knocked it out. He pulled a fresh one from his shirt pocket and slipped it into the empty chamber. Abruptly, he said:

"I ran beef. I had a ranch. I was a happy man. With a good life."

Slocum's jaw dropped. The shift in Dunn's mood startled him. It made no connection with anything that had gone before.

"Never went hungry. Never went cold."

What the hell? His life story? Just like that? Three killers panting for them and he was telling of his happy times. Of pumpkin days!

"Who the hell cares? This ain't. . . ."

"You want to know? You want to understand? Then shut up!" Saying it without taking his eyes away from the boulders below, watching the figures down there with a rigidity, an iron coldness. "I've got you here," the sheriff went on harshly. "Maybe you've got some right to know."

Slocum barely nodded. The sheriff suddenly seemed weird and strange.

"I told you I was a happy man, that I had me a

good life. And I did. That is, until one of them damn Vanners made me a grandfather."

"Huh?"

"A grandfather!"

It came out like a rifle shot, an unexpected burst from a distant ridge.

"You heard me! The one in jail. Lee Vanner. He raped my daughter!"

He jerked his head around again, his face fierce, his eyes fixed, murderous as a hawk.

"Raped her. Fourteen years old. And that bastard raped her. She's in St. Louis now. With the kid."

He turned his head as if he, himself, was startled by that sudden glare of killing in his eyes. He clamped down on the light and the sound that roiled within him.

"I took this job to get justice."

"But," Slocum said, bewildered, "but what about that sheriff. The one before you?"

"No damn good. A thief. Leaned on everybody for a lousy dollar."

"But they killed him!"

"He just squeezed them Vanners once too often."

"Shit, man!" Slocum was furious. "That's what this is all supposed to be about. The killing of a *sheriff*!"

Dunn shrugged. His voice quieted, settled into a kind of flat, private peace.

"Don't make no difference what they get hanged for. Just so they get justice. That's all."

129

Open-mouthed, Slocum stared.

Below them, Job and Chris upon their horses watched Billy's figure scrambling up the rock slide. Like a goat he jumped and darted, making for a stone ledge above him, a ledge that widened and ran along the face of the cliff. When he got to the ledge, he stood up. He waved his gun. Then he did a little jig. Then he put the gun down, flapped his arms and cawed like a magpie. Then, with his face opening, grinning like a wild weed, he lifted the gun and loped on along the ledge.

"You mean," Slocum said, saying it almost in a whisper as though he couldn't contain his outrage any other way, "you got the whole goddamn world involved, got this whole town in trouble, just to get personal vengeance?"

"What?" Dunn whirled on him.

"Personal vengeance!"

"Listen, you, I could have shot that bastard when I caught him in the Rio Grande! Look. I'll tell you something! I went looking for that Lee Vanner months before the sheriff got killed. And it wasn't for no personal vengeance! I was going to get him and bring him in! And, damnit, when they got the sheriff it was like a convenience! I could hunt for that louse officially!"

He grabbed Slocum's shirt and pulled him close.

"Personal vengeance! One man punishing another? That ain't what I want! That ain't justice!"

He shoved Slocum away.

130

For an instant Slocum gazed at him. Then, he took a deep breath and almost venomously said:

"You're crazy. That's it. You're crazy, too!"

The gun barrel was shoved under his nose. He could smell the grease.

"Don't push me, Slocum! Don't push me too far!"

Now Slocum was enraged. "Go on, shoot!" he yelled, his words echoing in the crevice like shouts from a crowd. "One crazy bastard or another. What difference does it make who gets me killed? You've been playing games with my life and with all of them in the saloon. So, shoot, you son of a bitch! Shoot!"

"Shut up!"

"Justice, he talks about. Justice! Horseshit, Dunn!"

The hand holding the gun was trembling now. Dunn snarled hoarsely: "Listen, it doesn't exist, it doesn't exist unless everybody's got a share in it. That's what makes it real. That's what creates it in this goddamn jungle!" The gun trembled. The mouth trembled. The sheriff's voice shook.

"More horseshit!" Slocum went blindly on. "I call it personal vengeance! And all you're doing is using us to get it!"

"All right!" All the trembling stopped. Gun hand, voice, mouth all hardened. "That's what you want to think? All right! Once a jackass, always a jackass! But, I'll tell you this, Slocum," and his voice began to rise, rolling and rumbling and climbing the massive stone walls, defiant in the wilderness.

"I got eight men. I intend to get four more. Twelve! You hear me? Twelve! And I'm going to get them sworn in. Afterwards, I'll deal with this not-guilty business. But first, I'm going to get justice moving. I'm going to get a jury sworn in!"

In the moment of silence that followed, Slocum felt a crawling, prickling awe, and when that was gone, there settled on him, like snow on a mountain, the cold, pure certainty that the sheriff meant it, meant it all. He glimpsed it for a moment, lifting glacial and white in chill air. Justice.

"Hello, cousin," a voice echoingly said.

It came from the walls, the stone, the pores of the rock. It reached up for them from hard-packed earth beneath their feet. It spread toward them from all sides. It sank down crushingly from above.

"Hello, cousin."

They both were paralyzed. And then suddenly the sheriff swung. The blow smashed across Slocum's chest and he went crashing backwards. As he fell he saw Billy some twenty feet above. He saw him straddling a split in the rock ceiling. He saw walls racing upwards and at their apex, wiry legs, breechclout and then the wild weed grin above the downward pointing barrel of a six-gun.

"Goodbye, cousin," the grin said and fired.

In the small space the sound was more than shattering, more than the blast of a single gun. It was as though mountain and rocks had exploded.

And at the top of it Slocum saw Billy's grin fade in astonishment. He saw a hand coming away from

Billy's chest and Billy gazing at it with wonder and disbelief.

Then, Slocum saw the sheriff, the gun in his hand, Dunn's eyes fixed on the event slowly finishing above. Smoke, thin and wispy, like the ghost of dust, drifted about him.

Billy, still amazed, still stared at his hand. Then he screamed.

"Chris! Chris!" and collapsed across the ceiling split. Blood began to drip down.

When Slocum got to his feet, the sheriff was already at the crevice opening. Below them, they could see the other Vanners, their horses moving nervously in and out of the boulders, and Chris, his mouth cupped, crying:

"Billy! Billy!"

"Call him, you bastard," the sheriff grated with satisfaction. "Call him!"

"The other one!" Slocum jabbed a finger and pointed.

It was Job swinging off his horse and running among the boulders, scurrying dark and furry as an animal, heading for the rock slide. The sheriff brought up the gun and fired. John saw the shattering of rock fragments as the bullet smashed into stone.

The shock was over now. The sense of being paralyzed, caught and trapped in the center of universal chaos was gone. Disaster had been in the doorway and then had passed on, and he was still alive. His brain teemed.

Slocum grabbed at Dunn's arm and pulled.

"A boost!" he yelled. "Give me a boost!"

"What?"

"There's a gun up there you dumb bastard! Give me a boost!"

Dunn stared. To Slocum it seemed the sheriff had suddenly become cold, heavy stone.

"What the hell are you waiting for?" Slocum was shrill with fury. "Another gun's up there!"

"Get going," Dunn abruptly said. He holstered his gun and made a stirrup of his hands.

Now elated, Slocum placed a booted foot in the sheriff's hand. He gripped the big man's shoulders and as Dunn heaved, Slocum shot upwards between the narrowing walls of the crevice.

The wall bulged above the sheriff's head. Slocum clutched at it. More than a bulge! A tiny ledge, a ledge big enough for a candle! He got his fingers on it and pulled until he had one knee planted on it. Then he jammed his other leg against the opposite wall. He reached up and for a moment was spread-eagled between the crevice walls. He looked up and he saw Billy's body across the roof opening. He saw the wound, dark and oozing. A drop struck him on the forehead. All the way it would keep dripping and he wouldn't be able to wipe it off. Only keep it out of his eyes, out of his mouth, he prayed. His stomach turned at the thought of another man's blood slowly seeping down his throat. Jesus! Keep it off me! And he started painfully, carefully, to work his way upwards.

134

In the beginning he felt as though he was pulling himself apart, from the muscles and ligaments in his thighs upwards, tearing groin and belly in two. He began to sweat as he inched higher, and the blood dripping from the raw wound above him mixed with it, and ran down the sides of his face and touched the corners of his lips. He could taste a saltiness and because he was breathing heavily and hard, he couldn't keep his mouth closed.

He dropped his head, and between his legs, through the film of sweat and blood, he could see the blurred figure of the sheriff, gun in hand, watching.

He strained, pushed, and as the walls narrowed, the pain crept down to his calves and ankles and spread along his arms until his shoulders intolerably ached.

Then he was there, just below the body. He took a deep rasping breath and raised his head. His head hit the body like a blow and, straining, Slocum shoved.

The body rolled. Sunlight flooded him. In a kind of panic, a near hysteria, Slocum grabbed the lip of the opening and pulled. His head, smeared with blood, popped up above the hole. He kept on desperately pulling until he was halfway out and sitting on the lip, his feet still dangling in the dimness of the crevice.

In huge gulps, he drew in air. Muscles, ligaments, that had almost strangled his heart, let go,

135

and he felt his body sag as though it was moving
dizzily away.

Slocum shut his eyes and shook himself and then
he sprang out of the hole.

Billy was lying face-upwards now on the bare
rock, arms flung to each side, mouth and eyes still
wide with astonishment. Feverishly, Slocum began
to unstrap the cartridge belt from around the
body, and as he did so the dead man became a
ragged, heavy bundle in his hands. He got the
buckle loose. He yanked. The bundle rolled face
downwards, over the crevice opening again.

The gun! Damnit, the gun! Slocum turned in
panic. Where the hell was the gun? Then he saw it,
lying a few feet away on the sun-bleached rock. He
ran to it, picked it up, turned, and his heart
jumped. Something was coming up over the far end
of the rock shelf.

Job Vanner!

He saw the rifle. He saw it coming up, sunlight
flaring along its barrel, as if there was a silent burst
before the real shot.

And the body! The body was over the opening
again! Slocum dived and at the same instant he
heard the shot. He heard it thwack into the body,
thudding into it, brutally splattering blood and
flesh. Wildly, he shoved. Billy went rolling. Slocum
thrust his legs into the hole and, gripping the gun
and cartridge belt, he dropped. As his head slipped
out of sight, the rifle cracked again.

He would have broken an ankle or a leg if the

sheriff hadn't caught him. But before he could catch his breath or feel the pain from his scraped knuckles, or even wipe the blood and sweat from his eyes, Dunn was shouting:

"Move! Out of the line of fire! Move!"

And he was being dragged, hauled, toward the crevice mouth and being shoved up against a wall. And suddenly the crevice roared and thundered and bullets were smashing into the ground near their feet, sending up spurts of sand.

Then the shots from above ceased. The sheriff, head cocked, listened, as if waiting for something.

The pain began now and Slocum saw the blood on his knuckles and he felt the burning at his knees. A dizziness again went through him, and suddenly he had a sickening feeling, a sinking of his own blood.

The cartridge belt! The gun! He didn't have them! He lurched away from the wall, looking wildly about him.

"What the hell you doing?" the sheriff barked.

"The goddamn belt! The gun!"

"I've got them!"

At that moment from the crevice above, from the rock shelf above, they heard the cry.

"Chris! Chris!" Job's voice sounded like a keening in the wind. "They got Billy! Billy's dead. Billy-boy is gone!"

Now Chris Vanner erupted from the boulders below them. He came out, his face a fixed blaze of rage, running straight at the crevice, his guns firing, blasting at a faceless, blind enemy as though the very earth and mountains had done this.

"Now!" the sheriff said and pushed a gun into Slocum's hand. "Now! Run for the horses. And keep firing. Keep him behind the rocks! Now! Run!"

And he shoved. Slocum came hurtling out of the crevice and, once again, in the shock of broad daylight, of being out in the open and guns firing at him, panic hit. He started blindly firing and running. He heard explosions alongside of him and he somehow knew it was Dunn. This time, as he ran, and with the gunshots shattering the air, he had the sense of being caught in an avalanche, a berserk roaring, bouncing, sliding down of mountainsides.

Above them, above the crevice opening, Job was firing, too. But the sheriff kept moving, shoving Slocum, pulling him, turning him, until abruptly, there were the horses.

The animals reared, but Dunn grabbed at the bridles, jerking their heads down.

"Get on, damn you," he yelled.

There seemed fewer gunshots now. Reloading! It glinted in Slocum's mind like chill hope. He clutched at a pommel and swung up. He landed in the saddle and felt a new terror. He was higher now, more exposed.

"Kick her, you dumb son of a bitch! Kick her!"

He banged his feet against the horse's sides and suddenly, he was bolting away. The landscape, rocks, cliffs, sky, tilted and lurched crazily about him. The ground, granite-gray, arid-brown, dust-white, rushed up, running like tidal seas. Everything was caught up, plunging by, in some frantic flight of its own.

It was not until he felt the splash and spray of cold water across his face that it all slowed down and he found himself pounding down the arroyo once again. Ahead of him was the sheriff, his horse kicking up the water from the quiet trickling stream.

Slocum rode into the cooling spray like a man crossing the border into another land.

After a while, they came out of the arroyo and onto the sagebrush plain. The sheriff wheeled his horse and galloped straight for the loma he'd come down from. When they climbed it and were in the piñons, Dunn hauled back on the reins and stopped.

"What's the matter?" Slocum came alongside him.

The horses spun nervously about.

"Damnit, cut it out!" the sheriff said, fighting his mount.

"Well?"

He got his horse quieted down and gazed at Slocum.

"You sure look a bloody mess," he finally said.

Slocum touched his face, his hair. Dust caked him. Dust. Sweat. And blood.

"That what the hell you stopping for?"

"No."

The sheriff still gazed at him.

"Listen, they'll be coming after us!"

Dunn shook his head. "They got a burying."

"Then what the hell. . . ."

"For this," the sheriff abruptly said, and leaned over, reached for Slocum's belt and yanked out the gun.

"Hey!"

"Just in case you get any idea about taking off on your own. You've got a one-track mind, son."

Slocum stared, first at the sheriff, then at the gun. His horse moved, jittery, under him, and it was like his own rage beginning to stutter. He had a sense of something strangling him, wrestling him.

"You . . . you son of a bitch!" he finally cried. "I . . . I just saved your goddamn life!"

"Thanks!" The gun seemed to have prescience. Its barrel came up. Its hammer clicked.

"We ought to be quits then! I done you a turn. You ought to do one for me!"

"That's a fact, son. And town is that way. The law is bigger than both of us."

Just pull the reins, that's all! Jerk the horse's head around, kick and ride, damnit! Gallop the hell out! It went through Slocum's mind like a remote anguished cry, like a distant memory of defiance.

"Don't try it," the sheriff said.

"You wouldn't shoot me."

"That's right. Jurymen are sacred. But your horse is not."

Everything in Slocum withered, slid down to bitter size, as if something unknown had humiliated his manhood, diminished it.

140

He'd die out there on foot and part of him was going to die there in town.

He knew this intuitively. He could hear it as a far-away, injured howl. And suddenly he felt alone and desolate under the vast cloudless sky.

"Move!" Once more the sheriff gestured with his gun.

Slocum wheeled his horse. Kicked it.

The animal began to gallop, slow, dark and heavy, bearing its burden toward the town of Blindman.

19

Job had carried Billy down. Carrying him across his shoulders as he descended the rock slide and then shifting him so that again, he was being carried across Job's arms like a child. Billy's head and arms hung down and the fingers of one hand trailed, making an aimless line in the dust.

They roped Billy to a horse then, and later, among the willows in the arroyo, they dug a grave.

It was twilight. And in the chill air they both wore their shaggy bearskins. Silent, monstrous-looking like some strange, barbaric form of life, they now stood thinking of the dead.

Crickets hummed and small birds, conscious of predators, hurriedly fled. The creek nearby tumbled. A star, a single ice jewel, glittered in the sky.

"Man comes to this here earth," Chris abruptly

said. "He comes with no rules, to live the best he can. To get satisfactions. To find his pleasure. To get as much as he can."

He paused, staring intently at the mound that covered Billy, gazing into it as if . . . now! Now he could see. Now!

"He only got a short time," Chris said. "So it ain't fair. Nothing should stop him!"

"Ain't fair to cut him down!" Job said.

"Ain't fair!" Chris echoed. "Ain't fair! Man comes alone. Like a bear. Snuffling at this here earth. To find what he can, he comes to live nobody else's life but his own. That's justice. That's fair!"

Chris stopped. He glared at the grave. Then, suddenly, he said, "You hear me, Billy?"

20

When the sheriff brought Slocum back, they had hustled him straight up to Robin's room. Gully hammered the window boards back and reinforced them with crosspieces, and now neither sunlight nor moonlight could knife through, and a lamp burned all the time.

His bones and spirit had ached and ten minutes after they brought him back, he'd dropped it all. Bones, spirit and despair. With his head cradled in Robin's arms, Slocum was asleep.

But now he was dreaming. His only revolt. His body was jerking, his mind flickering with images

142

seen in the light of explosions, of gunshot flashes. He glimpsed walls. All about him, gray walls and menacing, pressing in upon him as he frantically tried to scramble up them. And voices booming upon him. Then rolling away. And faces, glaring, grinning.

He climbed. He ran, and yet even though he got away from the walls, away from the voices, the explosions, the faces; even though he was running across open country, he had a sense of imminent ambush everywhere. A sense of trap. Of waiting violence and disaster.

"No!" he shouted and sprang up in bed. "No!"

"Ssshhhhh, honey. Ssshhhhh. . . . "

He whirled and stared wildly at the woman, his mind still plunging toward catastrophe.

"It's all right, John. It's all right."

"Where am I?"

"Union Saloon, honey. In Robin's room."

"Robin!" The panic drained away. He shut his eyes and leaned back against the pillows.

"I was dreaming."

"I know." She put her arms about him again and held him close. Her breasts were soft. Her breasts were warm. Gently, she rocked him.

"Dreaming about what, John?"

"I don't know. It . . . it was all mixed up. Came right into the dark at me." Abruptly, he pulled away. Sat up. Gripped the brass rails above his head.

"Something's going to happen."

143

"Happen to you?"

"Here! To us!"

"In this room?"

It was swelling in him, growing, looming like the walls in that dream.

"In this saloon. In this town!"

Robin gazed at him, a little worried now.

"Nothing's going to happen, John. 'Cept good food and a little loving. Nothing 'cept pleasure."

But he knew it. He was sure of it. It was coming inside of him the way the morning comes, the pale light becoming stronger and brighter until it was powerfully there, the blue glare of day.

Robin, with a pained expression upon her face, gazed at him, dimly feeling his dread and therefore dimly feeling her own. Then suddenly, the pained expression vanished and she laughed. She lay against his chest and caressed his face.

"Ah honey, honey," she said. She lifted her head. She kissed him. "You're tired. That's your trouble. You're just tired."

"Maybe. Maybe that's why something's going to happen. Here."

And abruptly Slocum sat bolt upright.

"Holy cow!" He yelled, and in his mind's eye, he saw Job Vanner coming over that rock itself. He saw that round, bristle-bearded face with its beady unblinking eyes as if it was a snake's head on a human body. "It was him," Slocum yelled, "it was him!"

And all at once Slocum was remembering.

144

21

An earlier time. A different time. Before he was in Wyoming. When he was drifting in Arizona.

He'd been horsing a freight wagon for a man down in Tucson, a fair job, that put cash in his pockets which thereby, in natural order, led him to the faro tables and the saloons in the town. An easy, uncomplicated life.

Only his boss had a pretty wife who sat at the front window of her house all day long, looking discontented and sullen.

And after a while she was no longer sitting at the front window but waiting in bed for Slocum, and the discontented, sullen looks were all gone.

Slocum used to tie up the loaded freight wagon behind the house, knock three times on the back door and before he could say "good-morning," was inside and wrapped in the young and greedy arms of a woman who didn't even bother to dress.

It went on for a month, and then one day his boss came home at the wrong time and Slocum in a wild, pantsless panic, raced from the house, jumped to the wagon seat and whipped those horses up like mad. He went galloping away while behind him a shotgun roared.

That was the end of that. At a place called Bowie he dumped the freight wagon, bought himself a horse and a pair of pants and drifted toward the Galinas Mountains.

He had no definite thing or place in mind. Drifting was also living.

He was out, maybe four or five days, and had camped for the evening among some sagebrush and piñon. He was boiling up a pot of coffee over a small fire when two riders came up. One was a middle-aged man and the other, a young kid. When the young one took the wide-brimmed hat off, Slocum saw it was a girl.

They pulled up and stared down at him. The man had a gaunt, tense expression, with heavy lines of worry in his face. The girl looked scared.

"Evening," Slocum said and quietly felt for his gun. But it wasn't there. Holster and weapon were draped across his saddle, ten feet away.

"Evening," the man replied. He seemed nervous, uneasy. "I'm Joe Warner. This is my daughter, Clem. We . . . we could smell coffee half a mile away."

"Well, you found it, mister, and you're welcome to some."

"Thanks."

They slid off their horses. The girl was thin, flat-chested, straight as a boy. Even though her pants were tight, she showed hardly any behind. No more than fourteen, fifteen, Slocum thought as she got two cups out of the gear behind her saddle and came forward with them, her eyes still big and scared.

146

"You from around these parts?" the man asked as Slocum poured.

"Nope."

"I didn't catch your name."

"Didn't say it. But it's John. John Slocum."

The three of them were squatting around the campfire now, steam curling from their cups.

"Traveling someplace?"

"Just drifting through."

The man kept fidgeting nervously, looking about him. His hand was shaking, slopping hot coffee over the rim of the cup. The girl's eyes were glued to her father's face, watching him intently, as though waiting for the next frightening thing to happen.

"I farm," the man said, "over at Horse Creek. About thirty miles from here. Bad year. No rain. Grasshoppers. Weevils. Well went dry, too. It's a goddamn hard time."

The man kept talking, staring straight ahead at Slocum as if the words really had nothing to do with himself, with what he was thinking. As if they were just spilling out to fill up time. Then, abruptly, he said: "Nobody around here know you? A stranger here, right?"

Slocum put down his cup. Something was wrong. Casually he shifted, started to rise, turning toward his saddle and his gun.

"Hold it," the man snapped, and suddenly there was a huge, old-fashioned cavalry pistol in his hand and it was pointed straight at Slocum.

"Clem," he said, "tie him up!"

147

"Hey," Slocum yelled, "what the hell is this?"

The girl hadn't moved.

"Tie him up, Clem! Damn you, tie him up!"

"A . . . a . . . all right, pa."

She scrambled to her pony and came back with a rope.

"Listen," Slocum said as she started to tie him. "What is this? I've got no money. I've got nothing. This is a dry well, too! So what's going on?"

"You're a receipt," the man said, "a receipt for fifty dollars, mister. That's food for me and mine come the next three months."

"What the hell you talking about?" Slocum screamed. The girl was wrapping cord around his wrists and pulling it tight, and she was terrified all the time she was doing it.

"Ever hear of the Tumbleweed Wagon?" the man asked.

"What in Christ's name is that?"

"Prison wagon," the man went on, "a big, traveling jail wagon with iron wheels that roams all over the territory. Sent out to collect criminals. Picks them up and takes them to the Arizona territorial jail. I'm going to deliver you, mister, to the marshals on that wagon, and they're going to give me a receipt for fifty dollars!"

"But I ain't done nothing! I ain't no criminal!"

"What the hell do I care what you are!" The man was shouting at him. "My family's got to eat and you're going to feed them for me! I had a criminal, mister. A real one. Man named Billy

148

Poore. Folks at Horse Creek wanted him delivered to the wagon, so I took the job 'cause I needed the money. Billy Poore! Had him in my hands! Had his delivering papers. But, goddamn!" The man stood up, the pistol trembling in his hand:

"He tried to bolt and I shot and I killed him. Killed my golden goose! Killed my flour and beans and bacon! But I ain't going to let my family starve. So I got you now. You're going to be Billy Poore and I'm going to deliver you and get my fifty dollars from the town!"

"You're out of your mind," Slocum yelled. He was all tied up now, with that cavalry pistol not a foot from his head. "You're crazy! They'll never believe you. Never, you son of a bitch! Never!"

The girl stood stiff and still and scared beside her father, and both of them together suddenly reminded Slocum of a picture in a book he'd once seen—madness and fear standing side by side.

"They'll believe me, mister," the man said, " 'cause I got papers and you're all tied down."

It turned out that Warner had to meet the Tumbleweed Wagon along the Gila River. They got Slocum on his horse, his hands tied to the pommel for added security, and in the first light of dawn they pushed toward the river.

"Listen," Slocum said, as they bobbed and galloped over the flat sagebrush country, "what did this Billy Poore do?"

"Robbery. Stagecoach."

149

"Christ! That's at least ten years behind bars!"

Warner shrugged.

"Look, let me go," Slocum pleaded, "take my horse and saddle and sell them. You'll get your damn fifty dollars!"

"A receipt," Warner grimly replied. "I've got to bring back a receipt. Otherwise there'll be questions back home."

No matter what Slocum said or how he said it Warner wouldn't answer anymore. And the girl, like her father, kept her mouth closed. It was as though the matter was absolutely finished, Slocum's protests shut out, the consequences of this act brutally ignored for evermore.

In the late afternoon they came over a rise and Clem reined in her pony and shouted, "Pa! There it is! The Tumbleweed Wagon!"

It was below them, waiting at a bend in the river. Slocum saw a huge, square-built wagon which looked like a railroad caboose on great iron wheels.

Four horses were harnessed to it and on the high seat of the wagon he saw a driver and a shotgun man. Nearby, mounted on ponies, waited two men. He saw them turn, jerking their horses' heads as they looked up when Warner's party came into view.

"Know why they call it the Tumbleweed Wagon?"

"Who the hell cares," Slocum said through his gritted teeth.

"'Cause it goes after criminals," Warner went

grimly on, "like the way the tumbleweed goes roving across the land."

"But I ain't no criminal," Slocum said for the fiftieth time.

"You are, son. To me you are, and to them U.S. Marshals down there, you are."

And Warner kicked the horses down the slope and as they trotted toward the wagon, Slocum saw that the marshals had their hands on their guns.

"Howdy,.Marshal. I'm Joe Warner," the farmer said.

"Howdy," one of them replied. "I'm Horan and this is Marshal Wilson. You delivering?" Warner nodded. "Christ, we've been setting here all day waiting, and we've got other merchandise to collect."

"Sorry, Marshal. . . . "

"Billy Poore?"

"Goddamnit!" Slocum started shouting. "I ain't Billy Poore! I'm John Slocum and this son of a bitch here, he. . . . "

"Shut up!" Horan ignored Slocum and turned back to the farmer. "You got his papers?"

"Uh-huh." Warner brought out a thin, folded sheet of paper.

And Slocum felt absolute panic.

"Listen, I ain't Billy Poore!" He tried to struggle off the horse, but the rope was too tight and he could only twist and yell in the saddle. "I ain't never heard nor seen this Billy Poore. This bastard bushwacked me! He's bringing you the wrong man!

Substituted me for a lousy fifty dollars! He. . . . "

"We said shut up!" And Wilson swung. The open hand caught Slocum across the face and he almost went down, around, and under the horse. "Just keep your tongue quiet and nothing else'll happen to you!"

Horan was checking the paper. He looked up and nodded.

"All in order. Here's your receipt, Mr. Warner. Delivered, one man to the Tumbleweed Wagon. All stamped and signed."

And Slocum still couldn't believe it, even as he saw prison doors slamming shut on him. Himself being shoved right out of the world and into a dark hole for maybe ten years. He started yelling again.

"It's a mistake! You're making a mistake! I ain't Billy Poore!"

He tried to tear himself free of the horse. Damnit they wouldn't even listen! His was just a crazy voice in the wind. Then he caught sight of the girl and her big frightened eyes.

"Tell them the truth, girl," he yelled at her, "tell them it's a whole lie. I ain't Billy Poore! Tell them!"

"Get him away from my girl," Warner cried.

"All right. Open that wagon," Horan said, "and I'll cut him down."

Wilson moved to the wagon's rear and Horan began cutting Slocum off the horse. He came down fighting, swinging both arms like a scythe, and shouting, "I ain't! I ain't Billy Poore! And nobody's going to jail me, nobody! No. . . . "

The last thing Slocum saw was the girl's eyes. Clem's enormous, fixed, and terrified eyes.

Horan slugged him with the butt of a gun and Slocum collapsed.

When he came to, he was inside the wagon, jolting, bouncing and rolling from side to side. He saw wooden walls and a wooden roof, and a window with iron bars high up, on one side. It was like being inside a small building, a shack, that bounced and rattled along. He heard the wagon driver shouting and the cracking of his whip. Dizzily he sat up and saw the other occupant in the wagon.

The man was sprawled in one corner and, in the patches of light that got through the high window, Slocum could see that he was watching him and grinning. He had a round face, a bristly beard and beady eyes.

"Welcome to the Tumbleweed Wagon," the man said, his voice rough, guttural, "I'm Job Vanner. They say they going to hang me. Shit mister, ain't no place in the whole wide world that's got a rope for me!" And he laughed, like a dog coughing. "What'd you do?"

"Huh?" Slocum was still dazed from that blow.

"What'd you do? To get in here?"

"Nothing," the word shot out of Slocum. "Nothing!"

"Just like me!" The man giggled and slapped his side. "Just like me! I done nothing. Just killed a fellow, a damned storekeeper. Hit him with his

153

own meat cleaver 'cause all he had was seventy-three cents in the till! Just like me! Nothing!" And again he barked out that laugh. Then, suddenly, he said, "Got any tobacco?"

"No."

"If you're lying, I'll cut your heart out, first chance I get. And, eat it!" And, he produced a gleaming blade from someplace beside him, and sprawled there, grinning, the blade glinting just like his teeth.

Robin was rubbing her cheek against his shoulder as he lay beside her, recalling that scene in the Tumbleweed Wagon. That first time he'd ever seen Job Vanner. Slocum lay, staring straight ahead, seeing Vanner's face in the dimness of the wagon and thinking, Christ, it was just like the face of some murderous little animal, just part way out of the dark, grinning and ready to tear you apart. And, for three days, he bounced and jolted with that hunched, collected murderousness, not ten feet away.

At night when the Tumbleweed Wagon halted, the marshals would let both of them out and chain them to the spokes of the wagon wheels. There for the night, hooked up like pots to a peddler's wagon, they ate and slept and breathed fresh air.

On the third day there had been heavy rains in the morning and the wagon plowed through mud most of the afternoon. Towards evening they camped in an arroyo, and Slocum and Vanner were let out and chained to the wheels with a sheet of canvas beneath them.

Soon they were eating their beans, Vanner shoveling them into his mouth, making whimpering animal noises at the same time.

Suddenly the shotgun man jumped up, his weapon ready, and yelled, "Two riders! Coming this way!"

The marshals had their guns out and nobody was eating anymore, listening instead to the thudding of hooves coming closer.

Then the riders were there and it was Joe Warner and his daughter Clem, and the father looked more gaunt, more desperate, and the daughter looked more scared than ever. Warner came off his horse in a scramble and rushed forward grabbing at Marshal Horan's shirt and crying:

"Let him go! You got to let him go, Marshal! You got to!"

"Let who go?" Horan asked, knocking the farmer's hand aside.

"Him!" Warner pointed to Slocum. "I done a terrible thing. I'm a God-fearing man and what I done don't let me eat or sleep. It don't let me have no peace. And I stand like the devil before my own child!"

"What the hell you talking about?"

"I sold an innocent man into bondage! He ain't Billy Poore! He ain't!"

155

Horan stared. He looked at Wilson. Then he looked at the girl, still on her pony.

"Your pa out of his mind?"

"No, sir," Clem said, almost stammering, "no, sir. It . . . it's the truth. That man . . . he . . . he ain't Billy Poore."

Warner grabbed at the marshal's shirt again.

"I killed Billy Poore. He jumped me, tried to break away and I had to shoot. Then I was in worse trouble than when I started out. 'Cause of the money, marshal. I needed that fifty dollars. So I found me a stranger. Him!" Again, he pointed at Slocum, "And I substituted him! Judas! Like Judas! I sold that man!" He pulled the sheet of paper out of a pocket. "Here! Your receipt, Marshal. I don't want it no more!"

"Jesus," was all Marshal Horan could say, "Jesus!"

"I buried Billy Poore. You come back. I can show you his grave."

All of them in that arroyo, the marshals, Warner, the driver and the shotgun man, Vanner and Slocum still chained to the wheels, the girl on her horse, and none heard the sound, the distant snarling, the savage growl.

Horan had turned to Wilson, saying, "What do you think?"

"I don't know," Wilson replied, scratching his chin, "sure sounds crazy to me. But it could be. Could be. . . ." And suddenly he stiffened. His head

156

went up. His face was abruptly taut and alarmed as he listened. Then he yelled:

"Flood! Flash flood! Coming down the arroyo!"

And now they all heard the roar, as if the earth had opened up and from its depths came a roaring, a bellowing, came blastings of air. They all turned in time to see the wall of water, ten feet high. It came churning and swirling around a bend in the arroyo.

Slocum saw trees and broken branches and boulders bouncing and spinning in that massive water wall. He started pulling, yanking on the chain, trying to break loose. Job Vanner was yelling, pounding at the spokes. The others were running now, the horses screaming.

"Free us!" Slocum was crying. "You sons of bitches! Free us!"

The wall of water hit.

The wagon was lifted up like kindling wood and there were rendings and splinterings, and suddenly Slocum felt the spokes give way and he was free, shooting through torrents of water, carried along like a feather or a leaf.

He slammed into something. Felt it. A man. And then he catapulted farther on. And all the time the air was filled with roaring and the din of smashing rocks and trees.

Then all at once the roaring was gone and the water stopped coming and Slocum found himself lying on the muddy ground. Overhead was a star-studded sky and a wan half-moon, climbing in the east.

After a while he staggered to his feet. A chain dangled from his wrist, at the end of which hung an iron ring that had once locked around the wheel spoke.

He gazed about him and down the length of the arroyo. He could see glistening pools of water, jagged limbs of broken trees and queer shapes and bundles that lay still.

He lurched forward and realized he was still in the arroyo. He began to climb its banks, struggling and sliding in the mud, and finally when he got to the top and stood above the sodden gash in the earth now filled with wreckage, he cupped his mouth and cried out:

"Anybody there? Horan! Wilson! Anybody?"

But the only sound that came back in the thin, wan light of the half-moon and the stars, was the clinking of his chain.

Dazed, he began to walk along the arroyo. All at once he heard a scream.

Slocum froze. Again, he heard the scream.

"Christ," he muttered, "Clem!"

Slipping, staggering, he began running. A pony, its eyes rolling in terror and neighing shrilly, went galloping by. Then he heard an enraged, guttural shouting.

"Shut up! Goddamn you, shut up! You hear? Shut up!"

But the screams, short, sharp, terrified, kept tearing into the night.

Then at the edge of the arroyo wall, he saw, not twenty feet away, struggling in the mud, Job Vanner and the girl, Clem.

In the pale light Slocum could see that her clothes were ripped and her thin, bony arms were flailing away. Vanner was struggling to enter her, rape her, his bristly face buried against her chest. The screams and the muffled, enraged sounds, and the struggling, twisting bodies in the mud was like a vision of some strange and frightened beast tearing itself to death.

"Bastard," Slocum yelled, "you bastard!" He grabbed at Vanner's hair and pulled.

Job Vanner screamed and went lurching backward. When he stood up, he turned and charged. Slocum swung. The chain, with its iron ring at the end arced through the air and smashed into Vanner's face.

There was a chain dangling from Vanner's wrist, too. He tried to swing it, but he didn't have time. Slocum slammed his own against Vanner's face once more.

Vanner slumped to his knees, his hands over his eyes. Slocum grabbed him and with his fist now, began hitting him.

"You better kill me," Vanner cried through the blood and spittle on his lips, "you better kill me right now or it won't be the end. I'll get you for this! I'll get you! This ain't the end!"

159

And, even after Vanner was out cold, Slocum kept hitting, until finally he had spent his own murderous rage.

When he let go Vanner fell forward. Slocum turned. Clem was huddled in the mud, her thin arms covering her naked chest, her body shaking with sobs. In the moonlight, bunched there, she seemed some battered, half-torn thing.

Slocum pulled off Vanner's shirt and gave it to her. And afterwards, they searched the arroyo.

They were all dead. Drowned, or smashed by rocks and trees.

Later, he found her pony and they both rode away. He took her home to Horse Creek and, after a few days he drifted on, riding north until he reached Wyoming.

22

"Honey," Robin said, "what's the matter?"

He was still thinking of Job Vanner and the man's cry, "This ain't the end. . . ."

Jesus! Everything goes in circles, Slocum thought. Rounds out. He gets bushwacked in Arizona, gets tossed into a prison wagon along with Job Vanner. Then a wall of water smashes everything and frees him! Then, years later he gets bushwacked again and gets tossed into another kind of prison here in Blindman. And, once more, Vanner's there.

Why? Unless something was supposed to get fin-

160

ished here. Something that never got finished in Arizona?

It was as though Fate had slipped up back there and was getting a second chance.

At what? All the way down from Wyoming Slocum's luck had kept running out. It was as though everything was aiming to get him here.

"You asleep?"

"Huh?"

"Asleep?"

"Nope. Why?"

"Well, I been kissing you and caressing you," Robin complained, "and you been lying like you was in your grave!"

She was on her back, her soft warm breasts bare. Slocum gazed at her. Then he rolled over and, smiling, took her in his arms.

23

"Two of them," the sheriff was saying, "Job and Chris. That's all. Just two left now."

Coxey, who was in front of the group, snorted.

"Job and Chris! The worst of the lot."

Dunn bit back his anger. He stared about him. At Judson and MacIntyre, and the others. They were in Coxey's house, in his parlor. Bunched around the marble-topped table with its heavy Bible, under the ornate lamp that hung from the ceiling. The light looked muddy on their dark clothes and hard faces. Greasy on the horsehair sofa with its doilies.

Take it easy, the sheriff told himself. Hold it back. Control yourself. You had to come up on these bastards as if you were just an acquaintance passing by.

"Still," he breathed slowly, "only two. Not three. That's less to worry about."

"So?"

"So I figure maybe you'll change your minds. That's why I asked for this meeting. Four more men. That's all I need to fill that jury and I can quit hunting. Maybe four of you gents'll step forward now."

He paused. Waiting. Hoping he wouldn't have to say anymore, that they'd see what the situation really was now. What it meant. That they were all crowded now. More exposed, trapped, imperiled.

"And, if we don't?"

"Then I've got to keep on looking for four more men."

He felt a spurt of rage. Goddamnit, Billy was the family favorite. He was Job, Chris and Lee improved. He was what they wanted to be. Faster. Deadlier. More reckless. He was the perfection of their wildness. Their image of God! What in hell did these clods think the Vanners would do now? Sit on their haunches and moan?

Suddenly, he trembled as if violence stood outside the door, ready to roar and leap upon everything in the world.

162

"Well?" It came out rasping, harsh. "You going to decide?"

The townsmen moved. They were like shadows muttering and shifting, handing a single quick angry glance to one another. Then Judson coughed and said:

"Seems like *you* got less to worry about now."

"Huh?"

"Two of 'em, you said. That's all. Less than three."

He stared, seeing only the lips moving, hearing the words coming slowly, like a kind of venom.

"That ought to make it easier for you. Safer to find the other four jurymen."

"You started this," Coxey said. "It's still your play."

"You bastards!" Dunn could hardly hear his own voice. It seemed suddenly so far away. "That's what you want, isn't it? To leave me out there all alone!"

24

When Job and Chris came out of the arroyo, high clouds had blanketed the stars and they rode across the sage not as dim figures, but only as sounds. Thudding hooves, scrapings, swish of branches, snortings of horses, abrupt curses, heavy breathing.

They climbed the loma, halted for a moment and

then trotted on. Later they halted for a longer time and there was only measured breathing, snufflings and stirrings, as in sleep. They were resting the horses. Resting themselves. They had glimpsed tiny lights hung far away.

Then, once more, there were the abrupt curses, the scrapings, the thudding hooves, again the fragmentary darting sounds moving through the night.

They came upon Blindman from the north. They pulled their horses to a stop and, shapeless, bulky-looking in their bearskins, they sat gazing down the rutted road through town.

Music. A piano tinkling. Voices singing, chanting. They could hear it, and against the lighted windows of the saloon, they could see shadows cross, shadows that hesitated, shadows that leaped and ran.

Opposite was the sheriff's office, and the jail. Its window was also yellowed with light.

Farther on, darkness. Darkness in the mercantile establishment, the livery stable, the funeral parlor. Still farther, at the south end, a light in an adobe house. But, darkness in the center, in the heart of town.

"It's ripe," Chris said, and walked his horse down the middle of the road.

25

In the sheriff's office, Pop was seated beside the battered desk, darning a pair of socks. He had his boots off and his bare toes were curled on the bottom rung of the chair. His shotgun lay across the desk.

Wizened and angry, he squinted at the needle and thread, watching them as if they had a dangerous, malicious will of their own.

The door to the jail cell was open and every so often Pop glanced up. Behind the bars he could see Lee Vanner sprawled on the cot. Lee was snoring.

The old man's feet felt cold. He rubbed them together. Then he looked at them. Chicken feet, he thought. Goddamn old man's legs and toes. Thin, bony, scaly. Callouses. Bunions! Everything! The whole thing! Blue veins, knotted and swollen. Nails shriveled, broken. Holy Mother! Soon he'd be needing bailing wire to hold himself together! He had age on him, knobby as chancres, as warts, carbuncles! He was studded with it, bumpy with it.

Snoring! He looked up. You bastard, he thought resentfully, wasting youth! Pissing it away! Careless with it like it went on forever!

He jabbed the needle again. "Not with him it ain't going on forever. That dumb bastard's gonna hang!"

Pop shook his head and laughed. He felt relieved. He was the lucky one! He'd gotten three times as far, and bound to go a helluva distance more!

Abruptly he jumped. There was a banging on the door.

"Hey!" His feet came off the chair rung and he grabbed at the shotgun. "Who's that?"

More banging. "Hey, Pop! Pop!"

"Who is it?"

"Sheriff sent over a bottle of whiskey!"

"Huh?" He'd broken the gun, checking whether there were shells in it. Behind him, Lee Vanner had half-risen on the cot.

"Bottle of whiskey!"

"Well, I'll be damned!" He snapped shut the gun and his face showed a withered spring as he smiled. "Now there's a considerate man!"

He stood up, put the weapon down, and bare-foot, hurried to the door. Oh, them desires and hungers! He was thinking with a glowing fireside pleasure. And he pulled the bolt.

The door exploded upon him. He saw bulk, the dark massiveness of looming bears rushing at him, and, just before it happened, he saw the faces.

Chris! Job! He opened his mouth to yell, but it was too late. A rifle stock smashed against his head. The fire went out. The snake's tongue snapped back. Pop went down, slamming into the chair and, for a moment longer, he did make more distance. But, then, only his blood was flowing on.

166

"Hallelujah!" Lee shouted. "Hallelujah!"

He had leaped up from the cot and was rattling the bars.

"Get the keys, damnit! Get the keys!"

Chris bent, rolled the old man over and ripped the keys from his belt. Job was going through the desk drawers, hunting for rifle cartridges, shotgun shells.

"It's about time!" The words came pouring out of Lee as Chris fitted keys into the cell door lock.

"Callouses all over me. Settin' here. Waitin' for you! Gettin' fat like a pig in a pen. Bet my pants won't fit no more! And cold at night like a horse's behind! And waitin', goddamnit! Settin' and waitin' all that time!"

A key turned. Lee swung the door back and came charging out and flinging his arms about Chris.

"Oh Chris! Brother Chris!"

He hugged him tight. Then he saw Job in the doorway, holding shotguns, rifles.

"Job!" He let go of Chris and hugged Job, rifles, shotguns and all. "Job, you old son of a bitch! Where's Billy?"

"Grab one," Job said and tossed a weapon at him.

Lee caught the gun. "Outside? Billy outside?"

"Shells," Job said and again tossed. This time, when he caught the box, he suddenly became aware. Something was wrong. He'd been doing all the talking. And the way they were looking. Like they were

167

here, but also like they were far away. Like they were familiar faces, sure. But just hung there, borrowed by somebody or something else.

He felt it happening to his own face, like it was separating from himself.

"Well? Where's Billy?"

Still no response.

"I asked you something," he shouted. "Where's my little brother, Billy?"

A pause. Silence like an abrupt hard freeze.

"Dead." The lips on Chris's face hardly moved.

"Buried him. Four, five hours ago," Job said.

"What?"

"Sheriff done it."

"And one of them jurors over there."

Lee stared. He gripped the rifle and felt himself being squeezed into it. He glimpsed a single rider, cartwheeling, leaping, spinning around on a saddle. He heard sharp and clear the whooping that always gathered his soul.

He felt himself harden into the gun.

"They hurt me!" he cried. "Those sons of bitches hurt me!"

"They hurt us all," Chris bluntly said.

26

Big Christy was still pounding the piano, and now, almost everybody was dancing. Even Sam Ely. Even Tex.

Only Meliton clung to the bar.

Damien had moved to the piano. His shotgun lay upon it and he watched the stomping and the whirling with his thin, glittering smile, his fingers drumming out the tune.

The men flung their arms. The girls spun in a shower of petticoats. They clapped. They laughed. Goldtooth shouted:

"Ladies to the left. Gents to the right!
You got one life. So do it up right!"

Buck cried:

"Gents to the left. Ladies to the right!
Ain't no tomorrow. There's just tonight!"

Upstairs, Slocum was holding Robin close.

In the confusion and tangle of limbs, in the graspings and gropings of their lovemaking, he saw and felt Robin's smile everywhere, felt the heat of her body, the grace of her soul.

He could hear the music and somehow it was for him. The stomping and the shouting, the song, all for him.

And then, suddenly, it was silent. Dead. He sat up in bed, startled.

"What's the matter, John? What's wrong?"

"It's stopped," Slocum said. He began to tremble. "Suddenly, everything's stopped."

Then they heard the first shots. It was as though the building had cracked open.

27

The Vanners had flung the doors back and pushed in and halted. They stood there, three dark, murderous beasts, faces yellowed, gun barrels slippery and gleaming.

The piano died. The dancers froze. And for a moment the silence was like a vast, soundless splitting in the earth, a jagged chasm yawning at their feet across which they saw their own torn bodies and bones.

Damien, paralyzed, stared. Then panic grabbed him. He seized the shotgun lying on the piano. He swung it up.

The Vanners fired.

Bullets smashed into the wood. Damien let go of the gun and frantically dropped down behind the piano. He saw Christy lurch from the stool, hit the keys, and as they banged discordantly, he heard shrill screams.

The girls were running. The Vanners were pivoting, firing all the time.

For an instant, Monty stood there, shocked, like a great tree feeling the first thud and bite of an axe. Then he grabbed at his chest and fell, smashing into a table.

Goldtooth was yelling, running for the stairs. He almost reached them, when as though clubbed from behind, he plunged forward, skidding into chairs.

Gully had gotten his shotgun up from under the bar. He was raising it, the fleshy, impassive face sighting before the stock was even against his shoulder. But he was hit before sighting and gun and roar could be put together. He was flung back against the mirror and bottles and in a clatter of glass he slid down.

The guns kept firing eruptive, rapid blasts.

Tex lay crumpled near the bar. Lola was fighting off Buck who wildly hung to her, trying to keep her between himself and the Vanners. She screamed and bit and scratched and when she heard him cry out and his grip let go, she knew she was free. She raced for the stairs when a bullet hit her.

She fell near Sam Ely, who lay stretched out on his back, his lips faintly moving, dealing out his last card.

At that moment Robin appeared on the stairs. She'd come running down the landing, a bed sheet wrapped about her. Behind her, still pulling on his pants, came Slocum. Their eyes were wild with disbelief.

Robin was on the stairs first. She came down them, the bed sheet streaming behind her, her hair blowing back, her face very white, thin, like the face of someone who had gone away and then raced back, driven by some instinctive terror and alarm.

Job saw her. She was halfway down the stairs. He raised the rifle and fired twice.

Robin abruptly stopped. For an instant she hesitated, a startled look spreading across her face. And, as it did, her face changed. No longer thin, no longer white. It was flushed now, rounder, softened with a wonder and surprise.

Flung against the bannister posts, Slocum saw her sway. He saw her reach for the bannister. The bed sheet began to slip to her waist and her breasts came into view and there was blood on them. Robin looked down at herself and, as if what she saw told her everything she had ever wanted to know, as if all the wonder was answered, she fell.

Slocum, himself half-naked, saw the bed sheet billowing, flapping, as she rolled slowly down the stairs.

At the bottom finally, she lay huddled, a small heap of sheet, body, blood and hair.

Chris grabbed at Job. "All right. Out of here."

And the three Vanners turned and fled.

Behind them silence came down, enormous as glacial ice and cold.

28

Slocum saw, below him, the bodies sprawled, the smashed tables and chairs.

He saw Damien rising from behind the piano, and Meliton behind the curve of the bar, eyes shut, gripping his knees, crouched like an unsprung scream.

And, then again, he saw Robin.

172

Seeing it all in the yellow light that was somehow like another kind of blood.

Abruptly he ran down the stairs. He dropped beside Robin. He grasped her shoulders. He shook her. I don't believe it. I don't believe it! went through his mind. We were just in bed. We were just making love!

Then he heard the sobs and cries. He looked up. The girls who had escaped . . . they were coming out of corners, from under overturned tables, from the back door. And he saw the shotgun on the piano and Damien staring about him gaunt and stunned.

Slocum felt a burst of rage, a tide boiling upwards as if something had broken inside. He sprang up. He charged across the room, seized Damien and shook him, screaming.

"You had a gun! You had a gun!" He dragged him from behind the piano, seeing Damien's face as a kind of blur. "Why didn't you stop them? Why didn't you?"

He flung Damien to one side, grabbed up the gun and broke it open, still screaming, still close to a blind insanity.

"Carrying it! Shoving it in people's faces like it was God! Like it was the Ten Commandments! Like it. . . ."

And he froze. Two shells dropped from the chambers of the gun. Both shiny. Both brand new. He stared at them. He couldn't find words. It was as though speech was enormous, as if this was the final revelation, the truth of madness . . . to see, to comprehend, to be totally aware and have no voice! To be without tongue in the face of what is stark and monstrous.

He began to stammer. He struggled, and he broke through.

"Bastard!" he screamed. "Bastard! You never even fired! You never even shot! Stinking, yellow, lousy coward!"

And he swung. The gunstock caught Damien across his jaw. He went down like a log.

Slocum whirled, the shotgun still in his hand. He saw the sheriff in the doorway and behind him, townspeople, crowding.

"He never fired," he cried wildly, "you know that?"

He ran at the sheriff. He saw the crowd behind him back up hurriedly. But the sheriff held his ground.

"Your goddamn watchdog," Slocum kept shouting, "your two-bit horse manure of an army! The man to scare all men! He never fired! He. . . ."

"Shut up," the sheriff said.

Slocum skidded to a stop. But the rage surged again.

"What the hell you mean, shut up?" He waved the shotgun. "Look at them! Shot down like they was nothing. Like they was tin cans on a fence! Like bugs! Bugs to get rid of! And that bastard never fired. Justice? Shit! You and your lousy justice! Judges! Courts! Jurors! Well, damnit, you've got no jury now! You satisfied? You've got no jury!"

"I've got no prisoner either," the sheriff said. He moved forward, moving closer to the sprawled bodies, the debris, the girl half-covered with a bed sheet. Behind him, Coxey stirred, inched nervously forward.

"It was bound to come to this," he said. "We told you so."

Dunn spun around, his gun in his hand suddenly, the hammer clicking, the barrel trembling.

"You, too! Shut up!" His voice was hoarse, his eyes murderously wide. "Don't say another word, damn you! Don't open your mouth for another word!"

Coxey moved back. Dunn was close to slaughter himself, close to pulling the trigger. But he took a huge breath. The engine of his rage shuddered, then quieted. He let the air out of his lungs slowly. His voice no longer shook. It grated now like gravel.

"You told me, did you? Who's fault do you think this is? If you'd done your duty in the first place...."

But he couldn't hold it. The rage returned, and the moment that he felt the trembling, he released the hammer and jammed the gun back in his holster. Nevertheless he couldn't stop himself from shouting.

"Damnit, you don't want justice! You don't even want the law! One thing you want! Your pocket-books and your bellies! That's your law! Fools!

Pigs! Killers! I'm surrounded by them! Drowned in them!"

He swung away facing the saloon, the bodies, the broken tables and chairs.

"Atensio!" he shouted. Meliton was standing at the corner of the bar, silent, dazed, hung in a kind of groping dream. He looked at Dunn. "Get out of here!"

Atensio didn't seem to understand.

"Beat it! Get a horse and get the hell out of town! You, too!" Dunn turned on Slocum.

"Get out! Take off wherever the hell you want to go! Get fat! Get rich! I don't need you. I'm quitting, too. I've got no use for you anymore. Or, for this, either!"

He ripped the badge from his shirt and threw it at the floor. Then he turned on his heel and strode straight at the crowd. He came towering at them. Again, hurriedly, they moved back out of his way. He crossed the portal, went down the steps and kept on going until he was inside the jail.

"Wait a minute!" Slocum suddenly yelled. He bent, grabbed up the badge and ran. Again the crowd moved clear. Slocum jumped the steps and ran across the rutted road. When he got inside the office, the sheriff was carrying the old man into the cell. He laid him on the cot. Slocum waited until he'd straightened up. Then he pulled him around.

"Now? You're quitting now?"

"I told you," Dunn said. "Get the hell out of town. Beat it!"

"Let them get away with it, huh? Shoot! Kill! Slaughter people like beef!"

"Get your goddamn hands off me!" Dunn cried, and knocked Slocum away.

"Goddamnit, you bastard," Slocum was close to tears. "Let them shits get away like it was nothing at all!"

"They ain't my load. Juries! Judges, trials! To hell with them. They ain't my burden no more!"

"Then . . . then give me shells! Give me another gun!" Slocum had his hands up, fists clenched as if they were ready to strangle, to murder someone. Anyone. "Because I ain't letting them get away with it! I'll go out and hunt them myself!"

"You'll what?" The sheriff stared at him.

"Hunt them! Hunt them myself!"

"Now, why?"

"Because . . ." and Slocum stopped. It wasn't there. The idea wasn't there. He wrestled for it. He struggled for it.

"Well? Why? You suddenly feel a responsibility?"

Slocum stopped for a moment and then, abruptly, he saw it. Abruptly, he knew. "I ain't going after them for that!"

"What for, then?"

"Because . . . because . . ." and it broke through like a faraway cry, "because I liked her!"

"Huh?"

"I liked her!"

"That whore? Robin?"

"That's right, you son of a bitch, that tart!

177

Robin! And, what's more, don't you call her no names, you bastard! Don't you open your goddamn mouth about her!"

"Well! What do you know!" the sheriff softly said, gazing at Slocum as though he was someone out of a half-forgotten past. As if he was someone dimly familiar, who had wandered by. "You've got a feeling for another human being. What do you know?"

"Listen...."

"Quiet!" Dunn's voice was again hard and crisp. "Don't say no more. Now, it's different. It's changed. You've got a personal feeling. A private feeling...."

"What?"

The sheriff crossed back into the office and took a gun and holster from a cupboard. He tossed them at Slocum.

"Here. Strap it on. I'll get us some horses and meet you outside."

Slocum gaped. Finally: "You going, too?"

"My God," the sheriff said, "how dumb can you be? I've got no load to block me anymore. You understand? I'm free to act! As free as the Vanners! To hell with all this crap about responsibility to society. To hell with it! I'm free to act on my own now!"

29

The molten metal of the sun spilled over the crests of the Sangre de Cristos and, far to the west, the bottom of the sky gleamed in the flow of burning light. Beneath it the sage was turning from a dark blue to a feathery gray.

Slocum and Dunn walked their horses out of a shallow wash and climbed alongside them back on to the plateau.

They moved quietly, without hurry, as if each was moving in a private dream, in a suspended, half-seen vision.

At the top of the wash they halted.

"Which way?" Slocum asked.

"Don't really make no difference," Dunn said. "We don't find them, they'll find us."

He swung up into the saddle. Slocum also mounted and lightly they spurred the horses and rode on.

Slocum still felt easy, unburdened, relieved. The slow, steady dip and rise of the horse beneath him gave his serenity a rhythm, moving him as it were, through a thinner air, as if he was drifting through it, further and further from Time.

He could get killed, he was thinking. Yet, somehow, it didn't have the meaning it should. It seemed unreal. It seemed as if it was another dream, without beginnings or endings, something that spilled like a stream through high mountain meadows. Pinos Altos, they were far away. Even Robin, somehow, far away.

They were climbing a rise. Patches of tawny colored sand showed in the sage. On top, the sheriff reined in and slowly surveyed the vast land.

He shook his head. Nothing. Then he swung his horse, bent and picked up something from the sand.

"Pottery," he said.

"Huh?"

"Indians. They lived around here for more than a thousand years."

He fingered the fragment of baked clay, turning it over and over. Dark lines of ancient paint could still be seen upon it, and the ridges of the basket it had been shaped against.

Slocum took it and examined the shard.

"What happened to them?" he asked.

"To who?"

"Those Indians."

The sheriff grimaced and swung back on the saddle. Under him the horse moved with a nervous daintiness.

"They met us," he said.

"Hell," and Slocum dropped the shard. He shrugged. "Everybody meets somebody someplace in time."

30

Across the great landscape they rode and Slocum still had the feeling of moving in a dream. Saddle leather creaked. Spurs jingled. Horses snorted, blowing away flies. The sun was hot and high and their shadows slid and darted over the low sage.

After a while Slocum had another feeling. That they had no purpose now. That they were only adrift, easily, gently, between earth and sky. Through half-shut eyes he watched the bland universe blaze and he vaguely smiled and he thought that it was warm and kind.

Still later, the sage stopped. They entered a canyon and climbed slowly. The sun was in front of them now and their shadows were behind.

There was pine and alder and aspen and the sound of water. The horses heard and smelled it and their heads came up and they began to trot faster. The stream was below them in a gully and, as the horses cantered, Slocum could see it flashing amongst the trees.

They came down around a north shoulder of the canyon, the sound of water growing louder all the time until it filled their ears with a muffled roar. The horses pushed through a willow thicket and suddenly they were upon the edge of a mountain meadow.

The sheriff reined in. Slocum pulled his horse to

a stop. Beneath them, the animals protested. They kept turning in angry circles, smelling the water nearby.

"Pretty, isn't it," the sheriff said.

Slocum gazed. Huge, old cottonwoods towered around them, and piñon jays, slate-blue, crested, shot between the branches. Water. Cold and swirling white, was cascading over a shelf of rock and dropping into a small foaming pool below. There were ferns growing on the banks about the pool and the force of the falling water made them sway. Blue columbine and gentians. Wild geranium and delicate shooting stars. Scattered in the grass of the meadow itself and amongst the blooms, pale, white butterflies fluttered.

"Isn't it?" the sheriff repeated.

"Sure is," Slocum whispered. "Sure is."

The sheriff nudged his horse forward. Still dazed, Slocum followed.

"Piñon jays," the sheriff pointed. "They'll come close. Haven't learned to be afraid yet."

They halted their horses below the pool. The animals lowered their heads and drank.

"Trout in that water. Big ones in the pool, I'd guess."

The muffled water roar became a high steady drone, a pitch of sound that seemed to John to be announcing something. He couldn't put his finger on it.

The sheriff was looking off into space and suddenly he swung off the saddle. His horse, finished drinking, turned its head, watching the sheriff bend, crouch, gaze at something among the ferns.

"Mariposa poppy," he said. "Most beautiful flower in these mountains."

Slocum stared at it. It was ivory white, bell-shaped, a single bloom with a yellow softness inside. Among the ferns it rose with a slim and clean grace.

Again, Slocum shook his head with wonder.

"You sure know the names of things," he said.

The sheriff looked up. "I know the name of everything," he said tiredly. Then, suddenly, he smiled.

For a moment Slocum had a strange feeling that the man was coming clearer, emerging, walking as though out of the shadows of the trees, of woods, of forests, bringing closer the meaning of his life and being.

Then his horse reared. He came tumbling off the saddle, slamming against the earth, doubling up with his hands about his head as the horses, panic-stricken, kicked and flailed.

Then he heard the guns.

31

What the hell? Frantically, he jerked and rolled away from the bank and as he came right side up, he saw Lee Vanner.

He was above the falls, knee-deep in water, gun in each hand, shouting and firing.

In the grass, among the columbines and gentians and the wild geraniums, stretched out and returning the fire was the sheriff.

Slocum grabbed for his weapon and, as he did so, Lee Vanner jumped. He came, spread-eagled through the air, crashing down into the pool with a tremendous splash. As the sheets of water fell away, he stood waist-deep in it, raising his guns.

But the roar wasn't his. The sheriff hit him.

Lee went straight back, bludgeoned into the falls, under the pouring water and then, down beneath the pool.

Slocum had his gun out now and he saw Job come plunging out of the trees, hair flying back, wearing only a breechcloth. Screaming, leaping forward, firing as if the true power, the real power, was wildness, was savagery.

Slocum saw the sheriff's body abruptly jerk and then he saw him lurch to his feet. He saw him stumble toward the stream, arms outstretched as though reaching for something. Struggling for something. And unable to get it because it was so vast. As he fell into the water, Slocum fired at another Vanner.

Job dropped.

Slocum twisted. It was as though he knew now from where it would come, from where it would rage and appear. There!

In front of him! Face to face almost. There! He fired just as Chris came out of the trees on the opposite side of the bank.

184

He saw Chris, sighted down the barrel of the gun, the foreshortened figure in breechcloth, long hair flying, the grass up to his knees, the flowers shaking in the grass.

He saw Chris jerk to a halt, his chest suddenly oozing, blood spreading on it. He saw the man swaying. Then fall.

Slocum leaped to his feet and he ran into the water, splashing wildly across the stream, firing, firing at the body of Chris. Firing, emptying the gun as if there was no other way to smash, to club the horror down.

When the gun was empty and the echoes faded, the silence came again.

The cottonwoods loomed. The water poured with its muffled roar, foaming into the pool.

And among the ferns and the flowers and the grass lay the lumps of dead men.

32

Slocum tied the sheriff's body across the saddle, covered it with a poncho and then, mounting his own horse rode out.

He led the sheriff's animal carefully away from the pool, out of the trees and down the trail until, once again, sagebrush was ahead of him.

He wasn't sure which way to go, but he could see the mountains and he knew that the town lay near the biggest one of all. So he rode straight

185

toward it, taking it slow and easy, not so much because of the corpse behind him, but because he himself felt slowed.

Empty. Vacant.

He felt as if he was his own ghost riding out.

But he wasn't dead. He'd come out of it alive. Still . . . still. . . .

It was strange. A shadow moved before him and a dead man moved behind. Whose corpse was he leading?

The sage stretched bluish, misty. Far away the mountains rose like a dark chain of islands in a becalmed sea.

After a while, he found himself thinking of justice. It surprised him at first. Then, it puzzled, as if it came to his mind by accident.

He glanced back at the poncho-covered body that swayed and dipped and rose as the horse walked. How had this third rider, Justice, arrived?

The Vanners were dead, but so was the sheriff.

Lee, Job, Chris and Billy. All dead.

But, so was Robin. And Monty and Goldtooth and Big Christy and the others.

Justice?

And he was alive. He, Slocum. But he was empty, dead inside. Was that also Justice?

The good and the bad were killed. So where was it? Who got it? Who had it? He couldn't understand it. He couldn't even see it, and maybe it didn't even exist.

Yet, something had happened! People were dead. And something had been done to him. He was changed. Different. Feeling as if he had yet to be born.

Then anger moved in. Damnit, the only one who talked about Justice was the sheriff, the dead meat tied to a horse in back of him. Only Dunn! It was *his* fault. *He* put it there, sent the idea stumbling angrily around in his head.

And maybe it wasn't Justice. Maybe it was something else? Maybe the sheriff had been fooled? Maybe? Maybe? Maybe?

The sun began to descend and when it was low and the sky was burning furnace-red, Slocum rode into town. He came slowly, leading the sheriff's horse up the road. Across its ruts, the long shadows of the portals had begun to spread.

They came out of the adobe buildings as he walked the two horses: the livery stable man, the undertaker, the proprietor of the mercantile store, women, ranchers, idlers. They halted under the portals, staying in shadow, watching him, gazing at the poncho-covered weight on the trailing horse as it passed by.

In front of Coxey's store, Slocum stopped.

Behind Coxey stood his clerk and they both gazed at Slocum and the poncho with the same suspicious, armed stare.

"Who is it?" Coxey finally, reluctantly said.

"John Dunn." Slocum was looking at them.

187

Jesus! They were fading. They were there and, at the same time, they were slipping away.

"The Vanners. They're dead, too." He dropped the lead he'd been holding for hours. "Take care of him."

And he jerked his horse's head around and moved on.

Fading! Who was fading? Them or him? Who? What was disappearing? He was on a horse. He was moving. Yet, everything seemed to be dimming in a kind of fog. Everything blurring. The thing that had been in his head all this time was now drifting away, heavy, like another corpse.

He couldn't remember what it was. He frowned. What was it? What had been?

He was passing the saloon when something moved sharply. His horse reared. He pulled hard on the bridle and when he'd gotten the animal down, there was Damien.

Standing in the middle of the road. Dark, impeccably dressed, his head and jaw wrapped in white bandage. His face was very pale, and with the bandage half about it, looked like a damaged mask. But in it, eyes glared.

"We've got something to settle," Damien said.

And Slocum saw the gun strapped to the man's side.

"Settle? What?"

"I'm going to kill you," Damien said.

Slocum gazed down at him. He did not move.

188

Both his hands still rested on the pommel. And his drifting stopped. The fog faded and all the slowing came to an abrupt halt. And even though it was twilight, he suddenly felt he would be able to see for miles and miles.

"Why?" Slocum quietly said.

"Get down, you son of a bitch! Get down!"

"You've got private reasons, too?"

"Get down!" Damien screamed and strode forward. I've got it owing to me! You insulted me and knocked me flat one too many times. I've got a right to my satisfaction! I want Justice!"

Justice!

And then Slocum knew, understood, like a blow, like a crack of lightning.

Who had it? Who got it?

Hell, Slocum thought, hell! It's like luck. That's all justice was, a matter of luck! Something up for grabs! Up for who can get it! A wide-open game! Ripe for the taking! Anyone's prize!

Gotten! Grabbed! Raided! Belonging to whoever had it in his fist in the end!

Saw it clear as daylight. As glittering as granite peaks in the cold air. Murderous and sharp as steel knives.

In Blindman, justice belonged to the one who was left standing. To the killer who was last in line!

That's who got Justice here.

Or, and the thought for a moment trembled in his mind, maybe anybody, anywhere.

He didn't even get off the horse. The gun came up in his hand. Before Damien could draw, Slocum fired twice.

And no one moved. And no one came.

And Slocum was left alone.

GREAT YARNS FROM
ONE OF THE FASTEST-SELLING
WESTERN WRITERS TODAY

JAKE LOGAN

INTRODUCING A BRAND-NEW
SERIES OF ADULT WESTERNS

J.D. HARDIN

"THE MOST EXCITING
WESTERN WRITER SINCE
LOUIS L'AMOUR"—JAKE LOGAN

Meet Doc and Raider, two Pinkerton agents
whose daredevil and lusty escapades will cap-
ture your imagination from the very first
page. Here is rip-roarin' gun-toting Western
fare at its finest. Order the first two books in
this series today and watch for more wherever
paperbacks are sold.